BETWEEN THE WINDS

Kaid McEntyre hates his father with a vengeance and blames him for the life of drudgery the whole family has endured. Nevertheless, when his father is beaten half to death in Flat Stone Creek, Kaid decides that he deserves some kind of justice. Unfortunately, Kaid must fight for justice alone. Lawman Ned Gorman and local hero Walt Gertz are determined to see Jerem McEntyre dead. But Kaid decides that the time has come to find out why . . .

M. M. ROWAN

BETWEEN THE WINDS

Complete and Unabridged

LINFORD
Leicester

First published in Great Britain in 2010 by
Robert Hale Limited
London

First Linford Edition
published 2011
by arrangement with
Robert Hale Limited
London

British Library CIP Data

Rowan, M. M.
  Between the winds. - -
  (Linford western library)
  1. Fathers and sons- -Fiction.
  2. Revenge- -Fiction. 3. Western stories.
  4. Large type books.
  I. Title II. Series
  823.9′2–dc22

  ISBN 978–1–4448–0791–2

Published by
F. A. Thorpe (Publishing)
Anstey, Leicestershire

Set by Words & Graphics Ltd.
Anstey, Leicestershire
Printed and bound in Great Britain by
T. J. International Ltd., Padstow, Cornwall

This book is printed on acid-free paper

1

The wind blew silently past McEntyre's ears and swept relentlessly on to God only knew where. It carried with it only red dust, hot and gritty, for most of the life-giving top soil had long since travelled the same trail. He wiped the sweat from his eyes with the sleeve of his soiled flannel shirt and fought hard to keep control of the anger rising within him. Why, he no longer knew, for the initial reason was lying buried up on the only raised piece of ground on the homestead. The sun was blisteringly hot and peaking as he squinted through the glare at the man seated easily on the bay.

'What did you say, mister?' Kaid McEntyre straightened up as he spoke and turned to face full on the rider who'd stopped some way off. The man was flanked on each side by a group who looked as if they were hell-bent on stirring up trouble, and trouble with their kind was only ever meant to end in one way.

'I said are you deaf, boy?' The others with him laughed. Ned Gorman's posses were legendary for their sycophantic stupidity.

'Now, Sheriff, no need to harass the boy, what with his pa lying dead back there by the cabin.'

'That what you've come all this way to tell me?' McEntyre turned back once more to picking stones from a furrow. He heard hoofs coming slowly nearer.

'Your pa's lying back there on the porch, boy. Seems to me you should be paying a bit more respect than you're doing.' The voice had sharpened noticeably. McEntyre already knew where his pa was and the state he was in. He was dead all right — dead drunk. Same as every Monday morning. Sundays had been lost days to his pa ever since McEntyre could remember. Ma and the kids went to church and Pa went to

Rattigan's in Flat Stone Creek and blew everything, or near as dammit, they'd made on the dirt farm, on drink. Kaid McEntyre could not remember a time when he hadn't hated his pa. But drunk or sober, it was McEntyre's business and no one else's.

'Things sure must be slack in Flat Stone Creek when the sheriff goes riding round sobering folks up.' Kaid slammed his spade into the dry red dust and looked the sheriff full on before beginning the short walk back to the cabin. These men were the first folks apart from the family who'd ever set foot on their land, as far as he could remember. 'I'll take care of it.'

'That's my job, boy.' Kaid stopped and turned back slowly to face Gorman.

'No it ain't, mister,' he said softly.

'Now I ain't about to argue with you, Kaid.'

'Good. Now get off our land, Sheriff. You're trespassing and I'm entitled to deal with that as best I can. Now, one against eight means I take the shortest route and that means you.' Kaid's gun was tucked inside the thick leather belt of his trousers; his chances of beating anybody on the draw were remote and he knew it. But a stray bullet as his own body slammed into the dust might just hit the spot and not one guy there thought he'd fancy taking the chance of losing his life on a nobody. Kaid's eyes were as hard as flint and as cold as ice, reflecting the blackness deep in his soul.

'You're a mean sonofabitch, Kaid. Always were from the day you came here. There ain't a pore that doesn't ooze hate. You're no credit to your dead ma.'

Kaid McEntyre didn't flinch and if the sheriff had expected him to, he didn't show it. Whatever was festering away inside the younger man went far deeper than any insult could touch. 'You're the first dead man I ever talked to, Kaid.'

'Get off our land, Gorman, and if you

ever come back, your law-enforcement days will be over. So as well as having talked to a dead man, you'll also have been shot by one.'

'You gonna let this boy talk to you like you were nothing, Sheriff?' For once the posse were unimpressed.

'Shut up! Kaid, we're going. Now you listen to me. You get back there and bury your pa. Then start walking as far as you can from Flat Stone Creek. Squatters ain't welcome here.' The sudden click took everyone by surprise, the boy's voice terrifyingly quiet as he spoke once more.

'Get off our land or I'll put a bullet in you right now.' The old Navy Colt that McEntyre held was aimed right at Gorman's chest. That had come right out of the blue and shock was evident in the lawman's expression as the tension mounted. But heroes were suddenly in short supply.

'I'm going, Kaid. No need for violence. Like I said, squatters ain't welcome round here and that means you.' Gorman wheeled the bay as he spoke. 'For this ain't your land. You should've gone into town of a Sunday instead of to the meeting house and listening to a soft-skinned preacherman telling you all to grin and bear it when the crops failed and the folks half-starved to death.' McEntyre's gun remained trained on the sheriff's back till the group were no more than the dust kicked up by their horses, his eyes still following their trail till the point-illistic clouds disappeared.

Somewhere along the far horizon rose the lush foothills of the Sephina mountain range. Even from this distance Kaid could see the green remnants of the ancient forest. Water and shade were there in abundance and he wondered why his pa had picked this godforsaken spot for their home. They were all gone: Ma and the children and now Pa, it seemed. Being the loser he'd always been, Pa had given himself and Kaid a few more years of worthless toil. And he'd chained Kaid too, in a manner of speaking, for Ma had made him promise to stay and work the land as long as his pa did. Kaid's eyes narrowed, a half-smile playing about his mouth as he realized that Gorman's visit had brought him his freedom at last. With Pa dead, he was free to go. And now he'd no doubt that that was what Jerem McEntyre really was — dead. Sunup wouldn't see Kaid McEntyre anywhere near the hellhole which to him, had been that dirt farm, Flat Stone Creek and all the land around it. He'd no horse but he'd walk until he saw a way of making a few dollars and then the world would be his to roam.

He shoved the old Navy Colt into the leather belt once more and walked back to the hillock that sloped gently, looking out over the cabin. His eyes shied away from the crosses that marked his ma's and the youngsters' graves. There was no need to fetch the preacher, for Rattigan's saloon had been Jerem McEntyre's place of worship for the past fifteen years.

There was nothing left big enough to make a box out of and everything half-decent was gone from within the cabin as payment for seed that seldom grew. Not that there had been much to begin with. Kaid decided there and then he'd torch the lot and walk away as soon as he'd seen to Pa. A few blankets to wrap him in and a marker. What to put on the marker? With difficulty, he held spite and resentment in check. Moving quickly he pulled out the one on Ma's grave and incised with his knife: 'Pa', below the one word already there, grudgingly adding RIP. Then he shovelled away the dust to what he hoped was an adequate depth of a grave before replacing the marker between them. No need to give prying eyes an insight into McEntyre family business. He'd bury Pa and the past and start living.

Kaid walked a fair distance from the knoll before spitting the red dust from his mouth, his mind now stunned by the sudden, drastic change in his life.

Why had Sheriff Gorman come out to the dirt farm at all? That thought surfaced through all the other conflicting emotions. It suddenly crystallized and he stopped, his eyes steadily watching the cabin. The sweat trickled from beneath his wide-brimmed hat and down the back of his neck but McEntyre stood motionless, unaware of it, under the high sun. After almost sixteen years of virtual isolation suddenly Gorman and a posse appear — Gorman, who was practically rooted to his desk or Annie's cook shop in town. What trouble had he expected from a dude who slaved six days and drank himself into a stupor on the seventh? Kaid's mouth was taut, his eyes narrowing. Pa hadn't been drunk when he'd last seen him. He'd been dead. Guilt quickly came and went and suddenly he wanted to know very badly what had killed him.

Kaid covered the intervening ground running and stood silently over his pa's inert body. The older man was sprawled now, not face down any more in the shade of the porch, where Kaid had stepped over him that morning, but awkwardly against the top step. Somebody's boot had kicked him there. Kaid bent down slowly, turning his pa's head so that he could see that hated face once more.

'He ain't dead!' Kaid's hand went rapidly for the gun in his belt. But the realization that it was a woman's voice stayed his hand. 'Might be soon, though, if he doesn't get some water into him and out of this heat.' Kaid watched the woman kneel down beside his pa, following the movements of her large, rough hands as she made to wipe Pa's face. But his eyes froze as she turned his pa's head round.

'He's dead all right, Mrs Grant. Nobody could survive a beating like that. Just as well he was drunk when it happened.' Somebody had given Jerem McEntyre the beating of his life.

'No he ain't — dead nor drunk!' She spoke matter-of-factly and began to wipe away the congealed blood. 'Best to do this while he's out of it. Won't feel the pain. Now, get him inside, son.' Kaid didn't move and the woman spoke again. 'I reckon having him dead might just suit you a whole lot better, son, but that ain't the way I work. Now either you pick him up or I drag him inside while you watch me do it. Either way, I ain't about to let him die if I can possibly help it.' There was no judging in her voice. Her eyes met Kaid's as she worked gently on the injured man's face and he knew she understood. How or why, he didn't know, but she did.

'Gorman said he was dead.' Had the sheriff come to make damn sure? Kaid's mind was in turmoil. Why? It didn't make sense.

'Are the McEntyres so dumb they can't work and talk at the same time?' Her voice was sharp and Kaid took the hint. He lifted his pa effortlessly out of the searing heat and carried his thin wiry body indoors. Most of the furniture was gone, only some chairs round a large oak table and a dresser were left where a family had once lived. Kaid saw it as Ellie Grant would now see it, impoverished and barely clean, the utter neglect it had suffered for years apparent to anyone but the inhabitants, who didn't give a damn. He placed his pa on the bed and wondered whether he wasn't in fact dead, for Jerem McEntyre's hold on life, if he had one, was very tenuous indeed.

'Why ain't he dead?' It wasn't a wish, just a cold question to a puzzle he couldn't quite fathom.

'God knows. Something inside just keeps them hanging on. Besides, there's hardly any life in him. Just a spark, but we'll keep it going until it either bursts into life or fades away of its own accord. Somebody wants your pa dead real bad and that just makes me all the more determined to keep him alive.'

'Ma always said you were a stubborn one.'

The midwife grinned. 'I've been

married nearly thirty years to a blacksmith who'd rather stay friends with folks than ask them for payment due. It fell to me to haggle for money rightly ours and my kids. That way we kept right on seeing the sun come up next morning, good or bad. The midwife business just helped things along when customers could ride off faster than I could talk. Get that pot boiling, son, and some clean cloths and some soap. Your ma had a good chest full of that kind of stuff as I remember. The time to use it is right now. We'll make your pa real comfortable and then leave it up to him. Could take days to go one way or the other, I suppose. Have you made plans already, Kaid?'

'Yeah, guess I have.'

Mrs Grant looked down at Jerem McEntyre. 'Doesn't seem right a man should work hard all his days and end up like this.'

'I reckon it was bound to happen some day. What I can't figure out is why Sheriff Gorman came all the way out here. Another drunk beaten up in a drunken brawl doesn't usually rate a posse.'

'There's only one thing wrong with that statement, Kaid. Your pa was no drunk. He never touched a drop the whole time he lived around Flat Stone Creek.' Kaid handed her the cloths, his eyes held in the grip of her own faded blue ones. Mrs Grant was nobody's fool and he knew it. Old habits died hard and Kaid voiced none of the questions that raced round his brain. 'Now ain't the time to go quiet on me, Kaid. Something's eating away at you, poisoning your feelings for the only kin you got now. I don't know what it is but I know one thing. You're dead wrong about your pa there. Now I live in the town and know what goes on there so you ask me any question you like and I'll take it no further. He worked hard for your family so you owe him that much to find out the truth about this. Maybe you've got a real good reason for hating him, maybe not. What have

14

you got to lose, taking an hour or two finding out the truth? He ain't going nowhere. If you're wrong, be man enough to face him and tell him. If you're right, take as much pleasure as you want burying him on that rise and move on.'

Kaid knew the midwife of old. She was like a clam. Had seen and heard it all in Flat Stone Creek these past thirty years and had kept it all to herself. He moved slowly over to the window, suddenly aware of the dust and dirt of the cabin where cleanliness and order had once reigned supreme. The mid-wife's horse was hitched outback.

'What brought you out here, ma'am?'

'Some guys in town said they'd passed your pa on the Decault Road last night, looking as if he'd been in a fight and had come off real bad. I guessed he'd need a bit of doctoring. Must've been a real strong pull that drew him back here. You?'

Kaid shook his head. 'Told him yesterday I'd be leaving soon — for good.' Kaid McEntyre had had enough. He wanted a life.

'Your ma and the children then, I guess. There's nothing of him. Where'd folks get the strength from to do that kind of thing?'

'If he didn't drink, Mrs Grant, why did he spend every Sunday in Rattigan's?'

'Don't know, son.' She kept right on cleaning the gaping wounds on Jerem McEntyre's body.

'Didn't have enough money to gamble for any length of time,' Kaid said after a while.

'Or go with saloon gals.' Ellie Grant had read his mind. 'Can't help you there, Kaid. All I know is I saw him walk out of Flat Stone past midnight, tall and straight and completely sober, out along the Decault Road going home. So whatever happened took place once he'd left Flat Stone behind. He spoke to no one on his way in and no one on his way out of town as usual as far as I could tell. Never did.

16

Whatever happened took place along that trail. John was up to his eyes in work nearly all night with all the traders in town and I was keeping him fed with soup and bread.

'Now, have you got any food in this place? For Jerem ain't gonna starve to death if he wakes up and neither am I.'

Kaid nodded. There wasn't much, just enough for a meal or two. 'You hungry?' he asked her.

The blacksmith's wife smiled. 'Yeah, and so are you. Now set to and make some eggs for both of us. That way your privacy and you can decide what your next move is in there without having to talk to me. But I'll need to know your decision so that I can make arrangements for your pa to be taken to our place if you figure on moving away right now. Can't leave him out here on his own. I'll get my youngest girl Lizzie out to help me nurse if you figure on staying put to sort it all out.'

With that, she turned back to his pa and Kaid moved slowly through to the big open fire. It was kept smouldering twenty-four hours a day, mostly out of habit for the days of cooking decent meals were long gone. Each man fed himself whenever and whatever he felt like but there was always water simmering to rid themselves of the interminable red dust. Kaid poked some life into the smouldering embers, filled a bowl with water from the large kettle and gave it and the soap and some more cloths to Mrs Grant. He cooked the eggs and fetched the plates ready for when she was through. He felt he was sleep-walking, his mind rejecting what she'd said to him. He'd seen Pa himself going into Rattigan's, sneaked out of the meeting house and had watched him go in many a time. It had fed his hatred week after week, year after year, thinking he was squandering their money, till he was a grown man and stopped the charade of going Sunday after Sunday to hear the Reverend B. McWilliams, the preacher, so deeply despised by the sheriff.

Kaid McEntyre had a very orderly mind. Nothing fanciful, nothing showy. It came from years of farming. You planted seed, the rain came down, the sun came up and you ate or you planted the seed, the rain failed to come down but the sun always came up and you starved. Even Pa's life, with all its reasons for causing hatred and resentment, had a rigid order to it. But now, if Mrs Grant was right, it hadn't. And that bothered Kaid. He'd lived solely to hate and despise, had been churned up inside by it and now the reason for it no longer made sense. The drunk who'd caused it all didn't exist — never had. So neither did the drunken brawl.

An ordinary fight then. How did Gorman know Pa had been beaten up if Pa had walked out of town right as rain? And why the posse? They'd accused Pa of nothing that morning, so why hunt him down? It wasn't his land, Gorman had said. He'd been right there, for with Pa still alive it was rightly his. But they'd thought him dead. Had Pa signed it away? Lost it gambling right enough? If he had, Kaid still didn't give a damn. He still wanted to torch the place and if Pa died he'd keep to his original plan. Kaid reckoned his best bet was to sit it out. There was no way anyone could survive what that man had been through. What were a few more days in that hellhole?

The cabin's now habitual silence was broken by the low sound of a woman singing softly as it came to him through the stillness and memories came flooding back as Mrs Grant's quiet voice drifted through to him. They'd all loved Pa except Kaid. They'd known nothing of Rattigan's — only Ma and Kaid and Ma never once spoke about it after Kaid had told her what he'd seen.

McEntyre business — always McEntyre business, and old habits did indeed die hard.

'You ready to eat, ma'am?' he asked quietly from the doorway of the bedroom.

'Just about.' She rose and followed Kaid, washing her hands in the bowl of hot water beside the dirt-smeared window. 'If you aim to find out who did this and why, you ain't gonna get far without a horse. Take mine.' Kaid nodded his thanks.

'Might be gone a while. I expect it's time I had a talk with the folks in Rattigan's.'

2

Kaid's sparse, hard frame sat easily on the chestnut sorrel as they slowly covered the five miles into Flat Stone Creek. He knew every inch of the ground beneath them having spent what seemed a lifetime walking it since their old bay had died. The more he thought about it, the more it puzzled him. Pa had gone into Rattigan's every Sunday for what? Who noticed and who cared? Well, somebody cared enough to beat him to a pulp. A man who died in a fight Kaid could handle. Happened often enough in Flat Stone Creek when the ranch hands came back from months on the trail with full pockets and empty heads. Kaid was honest enough to admit that if Pa had simply got in somebody's way and had died in Flat Stone, he'd have felt nothing. It was the fact that he'd crawled all the way back to the farm, home like a wounded animal seeking refuge, that got to him. Any living creature who'd made that effort deserved more than pity.

He saw the first few houses appear as Main Street opened up, the meeting house that had once kept a discreet distance from the lowlife of the town now flanked on each side by a bawdy house and, opposite, the ever-crowded Rattigan's saloon, which spoke of the growing money that the fertile land further up the valley now provided. Flat Stone was five miles from their farm but could just as well have been a million from its red dust and ever constant crosswinds. So what if it kept him in this neck of the woods a few days longer? He'd time and damn all else.

First things first. Clear up this mess, earn a few bucks doing anything that paid and then buy a stagecoach ticket to anywhere and he'd be free. Maybe even head for the hill country. It all seemed straightforward enough yet the sheriff's warning — 'It ain't your land' — kept bursting into his neat little plan. Whichever way you looked at it, Gorman had meant it wasn't McEntyre land. It was worth next to nothing but they'd lived and died on it and as sure as hell, Kaid McEntyre was determined he'd be the one who'd decide when to quit it. Sixteen years and more of sweat and four dead up on that rise made it their land, red dust and all, said only a McEntyre had the right to call time on it.

He hitched the horse to the rail outside the blacksmith's and entered to tell John Grant about his wife. Kaid felt thirsty as hell and looked enviously at the barrel of cold, clear water the blacksmith thrust the red-hot horseshoe into. The hissing steam just emphasized its chill and reminded Kaid of the crystal-clear well on the farm. It was the only water supply there but it was real sweet. Why the hell had Pa chosen a virtual wind tunnel instead of land among the foothills? Trees and shade and soil that stayed where nature had put it ready for seed to bring it to life.

'Ellie decide to stay on?' The blacksmith didn't break the swinging rhythm as he asked after his wife.

'Yeah.' Kaid watched the mesmeric action as John Grant fashioned the metal before him.

'Jerem ain't dead? Thank God for that.' There was concern there and a familiarity of tone that told Kaid the blacksmith cared. The Grants were that kind of folk.

'Not yet. I brought the horse back.'

'How do you figure on getting back to the farm?'

Kaid knew that that was the black-smith's indirect way of asking if he had any intention of doing just that.

'Same way as usual.' The McEntyres walked everywhere. 'Mrs Grant said you've to send your youngest out to her with the buggy in case it's needed.' A surly-looking girl appeared from inside the house that backed on to the shop and eyed Kaid openly. She didn't like what she saw, but Lizzie Grant never had.

'You got any food out there?' she asked him suddenly. They didn't come any more morose than Lizzie Grant.

'Some.' Kaid knew there was very little but he also knew Lizzie Grant wouldn't pay a blind bit of notice to anything he said anyway.

'I'll fill up Ma's baskets, Pa.' 'Some' meant 'none' in her eyes. Lizzie had a tone of voice that dismissed lesser beings out of hand.

'Best ladle out some of your stew for your ma and take it too, Lizzie.' The blacksmith examined the horseshoe as he spoke and, satisfied, he tossed it on to a pile of similar ones. 'Guess the boys have been living on eggs and jerky for a bit. Your ma likes stew.' The girl threw the remains of her coffee on to the fire and the angry spitting and hissing that followed obviously reflected her mood.

'Don't suppose you saw Pa last night?' Kaid turned his attention back to her father once more. He wondered just how friendly his pa had been with the Grants. Maybe they'd been friends in the old days before Pa had learned to live the outcast and had dragged all the McEntyres with him.

'Saw him walk in. Didn't see him leave. Can't help you there, son. Your pa wasn't a man who stood out in a crowd. Nobody saw and probably nobody was interested, 'cept Ellie, of course. Sees it as her duty to rescue folks.'

'If nobody was interested, why did all those men ride out to our place to make sure he was dead?' Kaid didn't imagine the slight hesitation in the blacksmith's swing that sort of spoiled the rhythm.

'Never happened before, I take it?' Grant was as puzzled as Kaid.

Kaid nodded before speaking. 'You go into Rattigan's of a Sunday, Mr Grant?' The blacksmith was no church-goer, Kaid knew that.

'Nope. Don't drink and don't gamble and I get all the company I need right in here by my forge. Again, can't help you out, Kaid.' But he'd seen Pa go in, that was for sure. 'That business with your pa probably had nothing to do with Rattigan's. Sure were an awful lot of cowhands passing through yesterday. Maybe Jerem was just unlucky. Some of those guys are just drifters. Cause trouble and move on before the law can get at them. They're hiring over at The Spike and The Triple X and those sure are big ranches. Maybe their *segundos* could help. Be worthwhile asking. They know the troublemakers, for the cattlemen ain't too keen on hiring guys with violent tendencies. Makes for a lot of trouble with the other ranch hands.'

Kaid knew he should have asked Ellie more about that. 'Mrs Grant said she heard talk,' said Kaid.

'Oh yeah?'

'Said that was why she headed on out to our place to help.'

'Your ma and my wife go way back. It was common knowledge this morning your pa got hurt in a brawl. Plenty of talk. Ellie felt she'd be letting your ma down if she did nothing. Besides, like Ellie always says, there's no harm in your pa. Ready?' How the blacksmith knew his daughter had silently reappeared behind him, Kaid didn't know.

'He gonna see to the horse?' It was more an order than a question from Lizzie Grant.

'He's gonna hold on to it till he's finished his business, Lizzie, and when he has, I reckon he'll ride on back to the farm and let you and your ma come home. Now get your gear and head on out there on that buggy.' The girl suppressed a comment she was tempted to make to Kaid with some difficulty and he knew it would not have been complimentary.

'Much obliged, ma'am.' They knew each other of old and he'd heard of her temper from his sisters. What little formal schooling Kaid, his brother and his sisters had had, had taken place right beside Lizzie Grant. She'd been clever, morose and opinionated since

29

the day she could talk.

'Your pa's smart. What happened to you?' With that barbed comment, Lizzie Grant clicked the horse into action and the buggy shot off out of sight.

'Pay her no heed. She was fixing to go help bake for the church picnic till her ma told her to stay put and wait for her call. She's mean as hell when she's crossed. Why don't you ask Sheriff Gorman about the beating? Reckon since he rode out there on purpose, he should know what it's all about.'

'I intend to.' But first Kaid would have another call to make. He gazed out at Flat Stone Creek's Main Street. The noise in the street was deafening to him, his ears used to the heavy silence or the wailing and sighing of the winds as they fought relentlessly over the red dust of the farm caught between them. Just watching it all, he already felt crushed in spirit amongst so many people milling between the cantering horses. His pa and their troubles were already forgotten — if ever even noticed in the first place — by the citizens of Flat Stone Creek.

'You picked a bad time to come into town.' John Grant shook his head as he spoke, the sweat dripping languidly down his cheeks.

'I should've stayed home and waited for them to come and finish him off, is that it?'

The sudden realization that maybe it was a known fact that he didn't give a damn whether his pa was alive or dead hit him. Had they expected him to stand aside and let them complete their business? Was that the price of his own freedom? Kaid McEntyre felt sick to the pit of his stomach that a girl from town had weighed him up and reckoned that, as a man, he amounted to nothing.

'No, Kaid, ain't nothing like that. Traders are drifting into Flat Stone now and with all that money and liquor on the go, things can get mighty rough. Gives folks with grudges plenty of chances to even old scores in the confusion and mayhem. The sheriff can't be everywhere.' But there were no old scores anybody had to settle with the McEntyres. Almost sixteen years of virtual isolation had seen to that. And yet.

'Mrs Grant said she heard talk. Did she tell you why she reckoned she should go out to the farm?

'Nope. Like I said, ranch hands were talking. Where she heard what alarmed her and what she heard, she didn't exactly say. Ellie's a law unto herself.'

'But you saw the posse — heard them talk in the street. The sheriff's office ain't no more than seventy yards from here.'

'No posse left here. Gorman rode out on his own.' Just then another drawling voice broke the rhythmic swing of the hammer.

'That I did. Now are you on your way West or back to Tennessee where your folks came from, McEntyre?' Kaid turned slowly and faced the sheriff and his deputies as the older man spoke.

'Ain't going nowhere now you're here, Sheriff. Saves me the bother of looking you up. And if you want to know my plans, it's to ask questions, just like you should be doing.'

'You might not like the answers.'

'Ain't got any yet. That's where you come into it. Seems to me if there's one guy in Flat Stone Creek knows what's going on, it should be the lawman.'

'Seems reasonable. What d'you want to know?'

'Who beat up my pa and why?' Kaid watched the sheriff as he pushed back his Stetson to reveal a broad, close-eyed face a weasel would have resented owning.

'Don't know to both. You finished?'

'What do you think?' Kaid watched the others as he spoke, all itching to put him in his place.

'I think you're damned glad to be able to leave that dirt farm behind you and start living.' Ned Gorman eyed the worn shirt, the cast-off Stetson and smirked at the guys backing him up.

'My pa ain't dead and while he's there, I'm there too.' The McEntyres were an easy target and somebody had had some target practice on Kaid's pa. He should have been as cold as the clay but he wasn't. It was a while before the shock faded from Ned Gorman's face. He'd made one almighty mistake and fear etched his features. Kaid McEntyre had nothing to lose and that made him a very dangerous opponent indeed.

'He looked dead to me,' Gorman muttered feebly.

'To you and the boys. Whose boot did the examining. Yours? Or that ugly sonofabitch who reckoned dirt farmers should be seen and not heard?' That description could have fitted any guy there whose job it was to back up Gorman.

'I never touched your pa.'

'Yeah, like you ain't made one helluva mistake. I aim to make sure it's the last you make, one way or the other. Who were the boys this morning?'

'You don't get around enough, Kaid.'

34

'I aim to start right now. Anything happens to my pa and you're a dead man, Sheriff. Maybe you were right about hate oozing from every pore. Well, it's gonna flow in your direction should there be any more trouble.'

The blacksmith dropped his hammer. 'My wife and Lizzie are out there, Kaid. Guess I'd best leave the business in Seb's hands and keep the womenfolk and your pa company at the dirt farm. I got a right nervous trigger-finger, too, Sheriff, always had.'

Gorman took the hint. 'My job's protecting the citizens of Flat Stone Creek, John. Nothing will happen to your womenfolk.'

'Nothing'll happen, full stop, Gorman,' added Kaid. 'My trigger-finger ain't nervous. No sir. Ain't got a nerve in my body that doesn't do exactly as it's told. Anybody ends up dead around me ain't been in no accident.'

'You talk big for a kid who's never been off the farm.'

'Thing is though, Sheriff, do you

believe me? Then again, if it's all just a lawman showing concern for an injured citizen, OK, you've done your duty and warned me of the consequences of hasty action.'

'Take my advice, Kaid, keep the gun in that belt and leave town.'

'There you go again, Sheriff. Makes me think there's a bit of a threat behind what you're saying. Now my pa was beaten up and you ain't told me yet how it happened.'

'You're making something out of nothing. As well you know, I've known your pa a long time. When he wasn't where he'd said he'd be, I went looking for him.'

'When was this?' asked Kaid, his eyes boring into Gorman's.

'Last night — out back of the meeting house. Had been causing a bit of trouble, bothering folk and I threatened to lock him up. He said he was waiting for somebody and would stay round back of that building till he showed up. Checked up on my rounds later and there was no sign of him. I reckoned he'd headed on home.'

'And the beating?' asked Kaid.

'He was fine when I saw him. Just whacked.'

'From doing what?'

'I ain't his keeper and Jerem McEntyre don't take too kindly to folks interfering in his business.' That was true enough. 'Guys were saying this morning he'd been in a brawl. Had passed him on the Decault Road early this morning. There'd been a lot of complaints about him so I thought I'd go and have a word with him.'

'And the posse that wasn't a posse?' Kaid's eyes slowly roamed over the others as he spoke.

'Cowhands passing through. Met them on the road out to the dirt farm and thought there might be trouble from your pa, so I roped them in.'

'Yeah. Trouble from a man who'd kept himself to himself for sixteen years.'

'Your pa was mad as they come last

37

night. He was ready to kill and they don't pay me enough to walk into that on my own.'

'Well, Sheriff, like you said, I ain't got nothing but time so I reckon if my pa can't rely on the law to take this assault seriously, then his son should get a little justice for him. Now I think I'm wasting my breath talking to you, but I'll give you some advice just to show there are no hard feelings. Keep out of my way, for if I find out you're involved in this, I'll be coming after you. And don't you forget, mister, you ain't welcome on McEntyre land. It's Jerem McEntyre's and you'd better remember that if you want to remain healthy.'

'You tell me where it is and I'll avoid it. That dirt farm will never be McEntyre land now that your pa's in no fit state to pay off the mortgage. You should listen now and again instead of shooting your mouth off.' Gorman led his horse away, slow and deliberate in his movements. Kaid smiled, hoping like hell he was disguising the turmoil inside him. He knew nothing about a mortgage. Always reckoned they stayed there because it was their only asset. He took a deep breath and smiled but the smile didn't reach his eyes. It was going to be a long day.

'You watch your back, Kaid.' The blacksmith spoke as he hurriedly mounted his horse but looked reluctant to go.

'I'll be all right. Enjoy the stew.'

'Don't do anything foolish, son. Seb Reilly will be here in a minute. Trust him.'

'Just going to have a word with the preacher. Now what could happen to a man going to the meeting house?' Kaid's eyes gazed out over the street.

'Best ask your pa that. Seems like he and Sheriff Gorman had a chat all right and the meeting house came into it somehow.'

'You ask him for me — if and when he wakes up. Ride easy and thanks for the horse.'

Kaid watched the dust clouds kicked

up by the blacksmith's bay till rider and horse disappeared from sight. If he'd seemed in control to the lawman, he was pleased for, truth to tell, his mind was in turmoil. He just couldn't make sense of it. What could Pa possibly have done that that posse were hell-bent on making sure he was dead. It was nothing he owned, for the dirt farm was worthless without a family employed there day and night.

Kaid reckoned the preacher was nobody's fool. He baptized them, married them and buried them and did damn all else in between. Kaid guessed that gave him plenty of time to observe the comings, goings and general shenanigans of the saloon right across from his meeting house. Pa must have been a Sunday fixture for almost sixteen years. Jerem McEntyre was built like Kaid himself, slim and wiry, fair hair fading into a picture of nothing in particular, ordinary and silent, making no particular mark on anybody's life — except that, at some point, he'd stepped out of character and it was virtually the death of him. Maybe he'd just been in the wrong place at the wrong time. He'd seen something he shouldn't have and paid the price. Must've been one helluva something, just the same.

Kaid looked back along the road the blacksmith had ridden. Maybe he should have waited till his pa had come round enough to talk. But they'd never talked in the last ten years — not once. Kaid had made sure of that. Until yesterday when he'd said he was leaving when the sowing of the seed was done. There had been no reaction and he hadn't expected any. Hatred boiled up inside Kaid yet again. That man was a miserable, stubborn sonofabitch who'd been content to watch them all die one by one. Kaid McEntyre was honest enough to admit now his vengefulness was not for Pa. It was his own striking out against a community that had gone on prospering while watching some of their own succumb, inevitably worn out and underfed. The sheriff had been right. Hatred of the human race did indeed ooze out of Kaid McEntyre's every pore. But there was still enough decency in him to need a cause to justify his striking out and, ironically, that old man was providing it.

Kaid's eyes drifted back to Main Street and the dust kicked up the whole length as the town went about its business. Nobody gave a damn that a man had been beaten almost to death around there, for Jerem McEntyre had been considerate enough to drag himself out of sight and out of mind. Flat Stone was as civilized as any Western town, which meant that everybody left the town to the cowboys when their pockets were awash with money and then cleaned up, counted the profits and got right back again making more money in the usual ways. Common sense was all that was needed and plenty of it. It seemed that the McEntyres had missed out on that too.

The clang of the hammer brought his mind back to the present and he left as

Seb Reilly took up where John Grant had left off. Pa and Rattigan's, Ma and the church. Apart from those, there was no real contact between the McEntyres and Flat Stone. Schooling took place sporadically and no one took particular notice of any absences of children on the very fringes of that town's life.

The heat hit him as he left the shade of the building and stepped out on to Main Street. It sent beads of sweat trickling down his back. It was only April and yet the sun was already beating hard on the dust underfoot. Habits of a lifetime died hard and his thoughts went back to what needed doing on the farm. Gone but not forgotten, he thought wryly.

'Heard your pa's dead!' The stranger's rasping voice bit into Kaid's thoughts as he crossed Main Street.

'Then why is the preacher sitting in his yard doing damn all as usual? One more McEntyre he can cross off his list — or did he do that last night?' he answered.

43

Not once had the Reverend Ben McWilliams appeared as one McEntyre after another slipped off the face of the earth. But right then Kaid McEntyre decided he was about to extract from that particular preacher all the benefits that had been his family's due. Four McEntyres had ceased to be, ignored by all except the town's womenfolk who were as mad as hell at being deprived of a mourning social afterwards. Not a ripple did a single death cause in the ebb and flow of the river of life that passed for humanity in the hole called Flat Stone Creek, except for the concern shown by the Grants. Yet here was a stranger commenting on Pa's death. The beads of sweat evaporated on Kaid's faded blue shirt and were quickly followed by others as he wondered what he'd got into. He had nothing to go on and maybe the preacher's was indeed as good a place to start as anywhere.

'He was a nasty sonofabitch anyway, your pa,' the cowhand added stretching high in the saddle. The distinction between Pa and the preacher was very fine, it seemed.

'Sounds like you're a friend, mister,' said Kaid sourly, his mind elsewhere. Kaid reckoned the preacher saw everything, heard everything and said nothing. They'd gone to his church for fifteen years. He owed them. That was how Kaid saw it and that was how the Reverend McWilliams would see it, whether he wanted to or not.

'You kidding? Steered well clear of him last night.' The cowboy's horse was buffeted on all sides as it caused an obstruction.

'He'd have appreciated that. My pa's a loner — ain't the companionable type.'

'Amen to that. That look backed up by that hunting knife saw to that.' What the hell was he talking about? 'So he ain't dead yet?'

'There's none of us breathin' that's dead yet.' Kaid faced the man full on, shaded by the man's sweat-soaked form. His pale-blue eyes bore into the mind of the cowhand in front of him. 'Do you live in Flat Stone or just driftin'?'

'Triple X, but I got a hankerin' to drift. So long, boy. You've got the same mean look and I aim to put the same distance between you and trouble as I did with your pa.'

Kaid watched the man wheel his horse round and they cantered off, vanishing somewhere amongst the crowds now thronging Main Street. There was something obscene about life going on, folks laughing while others wept as Kaid was doing silently right then, his gut twisted in guilt and sorrow and hatred. He should have envied that guy turning his back on Flat Stone Creek for that was what he'd always wanted to do. But right then he knew that the trail he'd taken that morning was the only one that held real freedom for him — if he survived — for there wasn't only one McEntyre death written all over him, there were two — Pa's and his own. For an insignificant man who'd kept himself to himself, Pa had sure made his mark on Flat Stone. For the first time that Kaid could remember, he allowed a mental picture of that hated face to form in his mind. But it was indistinct, a blur of impressions, that was all. Had he, like the rest of the world, already consigned Pa to lie beneath the dust? The sounds of the street gradually grew louder in his brain and his mind was telling him that if he wanted to finish it all off, then he'd better use the little intelligence Lizzie Grant had credited him with.

The preacher sat out on the porch of his house, not a stone's throw from the meeting house itself. He leaned forward, writing now and then on some paper backed by an upturned tin tray. His Sunday sermon, no doubt. That surprised Kaid for he'd always reckoned the fire and brimstone came out of a book. The hell-fire guy of a Sunday in no way resembled the lazy man of the other six days.

'Morning, Reverend.' Kaid swallowed

the bile that rose in his throat for the sake of his ma. Reverend McWilliams simply nodded, smiled and waited for Kaid to go on. 'Guess you've heard about Pa.' Had a look of shame or embarrassment crossed the preacher's face, Kaid would have backed off a little, but there was nothing there but a look of satisfaction.

'He never once entered the door of God's house here in Flat Stone.' A shake of the full head of thick grey hair and Pa was consigned to eternal damnation. Pa had evidently made his choice and a faint smile played around Kaid's mouth as, for the first time ever, he felt a little admiration for Jerem McEntyre.

'He ain't dead. Can't talk as yet but you can, Reverend McWilliams.'

'Sure can, son. What is it? You run outa pine for when he does pass over? Want me to speak to the Clements boys — first-rate undertakers, highly recommended by Joe Stafford of the Triple X — and get you a discount? Remember, though, they don't part with a single plank of wood without the money first in their hands and the Church elders won't subsidize non-attenders.' Kaid quashed the almost overwhelming urge to smack that smug face right then, but dirt farmers had one great asset: no money, no nothing, but they had a soulful of patience. This sonofabitch's time would come when it suited Kaid, when he'd wrung every bit of information from him, for nothing went on in Flat Stone without the Reverend Ben McWilliams knowing it.

'Got a feeling what happened to my pa last night went on round the back of the meeting house, Reverend, not inside it. So the story goes anyway. Like you said, Pa never did enter it and you should know. I reckon you see or hear most everything that goes on round these parts.'

'Things happen here I've no control over — especially behind the meeting house after dark.' The reverend shook his head decisively and with more than

49

a little disapproval.

'So who did you see there? Pa?'

'Never saw your pa at all last night. Was called out to the Triple X. The old grandma was on her last legs and wanted comfort from the Good Book.'

'Seems there are a lot of dead folks hereabouts, Reverend, but my pa ain't one of them. Now I'd just like a quiet word with whoever he was last with and then I'll be on my way.' The silence was deafening. The smug look remained set on the preacher's face but was gradually replaced by his habitual long-suffering look reserved for the slow-witted.

'I never saw your pa, son. If he came into Flat Stone, I never saw him. Drunk or sober.'

'All right, Reverend, I accept that. But what's beginning to puzzle me is that you're telling me you sometimes did see him drunk or sober.' Kaid's dusty boot settled down deliberately on the bench right beside the preacher's heavy black worsted suit.

The look on McWilliams's face subtly changed from disgust to fear as the nineteen-year-old farm-boy's icy gaze with its complete lack of feeling bore into his own eyes.

'Yeah.' That was as much as the preacher allowed himself to say.

'Well, now, I'm not sure why you should think he was ever drunk.'

'You yourself complained loudly and often enough about it. Bawlin' after him about it in the street! He should've cracked your jaw instead of pacifying you.'

'I was a kid of eight at the time.'

'Kid or no kid, he should have taken his belt to you right there on Main Street.'

Kaid swallowed his growing anger with difficulty. 'Is that what the sheriff told you? Jerem McEntyre, the local pauper, was in a drunken brawl? Is that the official line? The one I've to swallow hook, line and sinker? You and Gorman real close on this one, are you? You see nothing and he does nothing? Is that

51

how it is? Well it won't do this time for I now know that being all day in Rattigan's don't make a man a drunk and more to the point, don't make his children half-witted. Now I've been told that my pa never touched the stuff. There's them that link poverty with stupidity but that's folks who don't know any better and it's a lesson Flat Stone should be taught.'

'By you?' The preacher barely managed to smother a laugh.

'Yeah, by me.' Kaid, too, laughed quietly at the thought. Lizzie Grant would have been highly amused in her own depressed fashion. 'So, any more to add that'll get my foot off this bench and you back to your wife in one piece?'

'Are you threatening me, boy?' blustered the preacher as sweat now broke out on his forehead.

'I am — and by the time your prayers for help have been answered, that assistant of yours will have been rapidly promoted to your job and you to glory.

Simple question, straightforward answer. Did you see Pa last night and if so, who was he with?'

'I never saw him.'

'You ain't telling the whole truth — I can see it in your eyes, Reverend. OK, maybe you didn't exactly see him. So what did you hear, then?' Kaid knew he'd hit the spot. The preacher moistened his lips and his blustering voice dropped. His eyes were now fixed on Rattigan's saloon across the way.

'I heard Jerem's voice, that's all.'

'Where was Pa?'

'Over there by Rattigan's. In the alley alongside the saloon.'

'Saying what?'

'Couldn't make it out. Your pa's got a soft voice, even when it's raised. Doesn't travel. Besides, there was too much going on with all the drifters and ranch hands taking over the street. Was just luck I heard your pa shout.'

'So who else did you see going back there?'

'One of the mountain men, a young

one. One of the group that always camps by Big Bluff when they're down off the Sephinas. Well, he didn't exactly go back there. He sat on his horse just off the street.'

'Think hard, Reverend. The shout — what was it?'

'Jerem had a knife out and was threatening the mountain man with it. Just sounded very angry.' Kaid's eyes narrowed.

'My pa ain't never carried a knife.'

'He did last night, son.'

'And the mountain man? What did he do?'

'He was real mad too, yelling back that he'd kill him. Began to dismount but I guess that knife persuaded him otherwise and he just rode off.'

'And Pa?'

'I saw him only for a second or two once he'd come out of the gloom back there. Your pa just sat down on the saloon steps. I had to see to the old lady out at the Triple X so I left town then.'

'That it?'

The preacher nodded warily. 'I don't know what went on later. My congregation wouldn't want me mixed up in the kind of things that happen round here after dark. I heard later your pa had been in a fight and had come off worst. Didn't surprise me after how he was acting. Somebody was bound to shut him up. He was as mean as hell and looking for trouble.'

'Well, he sure found it.' Kaid removed his boot from the bench and straightened up. 'Thanks, Reverend.'

'Now don't you go doing anything foolish,' McWilliams warned, 'for this is a peaceable town.'

'Is it now? My pa might just see it differently. I'll be back, preacher, and this time you'll tell me all you know or you'll be laid out in your own churchyard and I'll be the first to throw dirt over you.' Even as he spoke, Kaid's eyes were searching the street for the mountain man.

3

The only connection that the McEntyres had with Rattigan's was through Pa's presence every Sunday since God knows when. If he didn't drink, how'd he managed to spend every hour of the Sabbath in there? The guys who ran that saloon were tough, real tough; a dirt farmer occupying a seat for just spectating would definitely not be welcome and they'd make sure he knew it. So what the hell had he been doing? Kaid glanced along the street, half-expecting to see the Grants return, for the chances of his pa remaining alive for any length of time were remote. But the blacksmith's premises still rang to the hammering of Seb Reilly and Kaid knew it mattered not a whit whether Jerem McEntyre lay dead or alive in the clean bed Mrs Grant had rigged up for him, because Kaid had set his sights firmly on giving Flat Stone a last hurrah from the McEntyres; one they'd remember hereabouts long after the wind would have blown away all trace of the family who'd rotted there. He was nineteen and had never once been inside a saloon. Kaid wet his lips a little nervously and knew he was in for a hard time.

'Heard your pa's dead!'

Kaid slowed down in the middle of the street. The speaker sat astride the bay, tall and straight and stinking of sweat more than most in a town where sweat was the predominant smell. Kaid recognized him as the one with the loud mouth out at the farm. The wind that streamed through the farm kept it fresh, and at that moment a strange longing for its space rose up within him, which he neither wanted nor needed.

'You been out again making sure?' The man's gunbelt hung easily and Kaid had the feeling that Lizzie Grant was about to be proved right. More men had lost their lives on that very street from an overdose of smart talk than from anything else. But he had no intention of preceding nor following Pa that day to the next world, so he kept right on walking to Rattigan's. The silence, though, reassured him that his pa was still hanging in there. The batwings swung and he quickly summed up the clients of that particular establishment. Drifters, drunks and, more interestingly, mountain men.

'Don't make no payouts to deceased employees' dependants!' The man everybody in Flat Stone knew as Walt Gertz, the manager of Rattigan's, laughed at his own joke which was also evidently enjoyed by the clientele lounging along the bar. Kaid appreciated it as well, for it gave him the advantage of now knowing why Pa had been there. He'd worked there. He thrust the thought aside that yet again he had really no idea who this man they'd all called Pa really was.

'My pa ain't dead. Just so as you don't all feel you have to express your sorrow individually. Saves time. What I want to know is, who's got his job?' What job? God Almighty! He was wallowing in ignorance! He hoped his face didn't reflect his thoughts. This time the barkeep found his voice.

'Nobody. Walt here's just heard slavery's been abolished.' The sniggering sounded again. Something died in Kaid McEntyre right then. His mind once more attempted to conjure up a picture of his pa and this time it succeeded. Old, haggard, skeletal yet still burning with a glimmer of spirit deep within that soul, it seemed.

'He resigned — in a manner of speaking.' Gertz asserted his authority and the right as manager to speak first at all times in the saloon. 'Came in last night mean as hell and took the direct route out, courtesy of a few of the boys. Nothing heavy, though, so don't jump to conclusions, boy. The sheriff saw it all.'

'Where's the knife?' Pa's own knife was where it had always been — in the old box back at the farm. Kaid had seen it there that morning. Where had he got the other one from?

'Didn't pull one in here or he'd be dead for sure.' That rang true. What knife had the preacher seen? Suddenly Kaid stumbled forward a little as a huge figure slipped past him through the batwings, the slightest brush of the stranger's muscled bulk forcing the farm boy out of the doorway and further into the saloon. He watched as the big man, lean and hard, joined his fellow mountain men at a corner table. Tough as hell, they were, and taciturn with strangers by all accounts, but that man had crossed the floor with the fascinating stealth of a mountain lion. A hunter — but had one of them figured on hunting Pa?

Kaid's eyes watched them intently, drinking in their quiet talk, their easiness in each other's company, the invisible, impenetrable barriers they'd erected between themselves and the drunks, drifters and general loud-mouths around them. Kaid felt an immediate bond and could understand their need for isolation. His had been thrust upon him but he was by no means certain he wouldn't have opted for it himself.

'Why did my pa come in here if he wasn't working?' Gertz was the main man and Kaid addressed him once more.

'Beats me. Like I said, he just quit. I ain't his keeper.' His contempt for another McEntyre laced his words and he glanced meaningfully towards the hired help placed at strategic points about the saloon.

'How do you know he was as mean as hell? What did he do? What did he say?' Kaid could read the signs. Trouble was coming his way but he knew no other way to get his answer.

'Do you want a drink, boy, or are you goin' out that door the same way your pa did?' Gertz nodded to the guys closest to Kaid and they made no effort to disguise their intention to sort out yet another McEntyre too dumb to keep his mouth shut.

'Answer the boy!' The silence that followed the mountain man's steely contribution to the conversation was deafening. Which of them had uttered those words was hard to tell as the hunters continued their card-game in their own silent fashion. But Kaid's eyes were riveted on Gertz's face, which was rapidly draining of colour. The man's eyes darted around the saloon in a desperate plea for help as he found himself the object of the undisguised threat that had laced the hunter's words. He received none.

As if on an unseen signal, the mountain men hesitated momentarily between deals and all eyes were focused hard and cold on Walt. Being the saloon manager at Rattigan's was one thing, being dead quite another. If Walt Gertz was occasionally reckless, he was certainly not stupid and the words just poured out like a flowing tide. He spoke more to the hunters than to Kaid, his eyes glancing occasionally in his direction.

'Just prowled in and out of the back rooms mumbling that he'd kill him.' Gertz tried hard to shrug nonchalantly and failed miserably. 'That was it. Didn't say who. Just kept pushing past folks. Liable to irritate and get himself hurt so I had the boys put him out for his own good.' He glanced back and forth from Kaid to the mountain men, trying unsuccessfully to summon the look of a good Samaritan.

'Caring community, that's Flat Stone Creek all right,' agreed Kaid sarcastically.

Gertz looked quickly over at the mountainmen's table, fear etched in the brown eyes as Kaid spoke yet again. 'Come on, speculate.' Kaid intended making full use of this unexpected help, all thoughts of the unknown reason for it thrust to the back of his mind. He'd deal with that later. A faint suspicion that the last thing he might want them

63

to know was Pa's reason for being in Flat Stone was brutally crushed as his own icy eyes bore into Gertz who was evidently just as puzzled as Kaid. Walt Gertz shook his head.

'No idea, I swear it.' The sweat was beading on his broad face as he spoke, his sparse brown hair sticking to his scalp.

'An educated guess,' encouraged an unsmiling Kaid.

'Guesses get men killed, son,' said Gertz with feeling. 'You don't know how it is. You've spent all your life out on that dirt farm well away from reality.'

'Yeah, and likely living to a ripe old age — like the rest of my folks. Sure, friend, I don't know how difficult life can be in the big world. Lucky me, eh?' But the sarcasm bypassed the bar manager as the mountain men now silently gathered up the cards and prepared to rise. Panic invaded both Gertz's mind and body.

'Just said he was finally free to act.

Nothing left to lose.'

'Now that's one hell of an advance on just muttering.' Kaid was aware that the mountain men had relaxed again. He hoped to God they hadn't lost interest, for he knew that deep down Gertz was as mad as hell and Kaid himself would pay the price one day for this humiliation.

'You gents want some more drinks?' Gertz called over to them, his voice quivering slightly with anxiety. 'Sandy!' The barman moved fast to cement the peace treaty about to be signed and Gertz's breathing eased marginally, though he was still the object of the attention of the card-players. He'd said enough to keep them happy — he hoped. His hopes were short-lived.

'You ain't apologized to the boy yet.' The voice was deep and authoritative and devoid of any trace of feeling. The one who spoke was the oldest of the hunters but still in his prime, lean and fine-featured, exuding nerves of steel.

'Eh?' Gertz swallowed and choked noisily on his own saliva as the stranger spoke yet again.

'Belittling folks ain't neighbourly, and as you yourself said, his pa once worked right alongside you.' The man looked as if he could kill with his bare hands faster than any bullet and would trap a man in preference to an animal. Fear robbed Gertz of speech for a while and the heavy silence seemed to leach out into the street itself.

'Meant no harm, son.' Gertz's right hand sought and found the support of the bar as he spoke and thus he remained upright.

'Then I suggest the boy leaves — unescorted.' The hunter's eyes slowly left Gertz's exhausted features and Kaid's slight nod of the head acknowledged good advice and his gratitude for their help. He backed out slowly and emerged into the cool shaded porch before heading quickly back along the street to the blacksmith's. He had to think this out and he'd do it best on his own. He had to eat, too. The McEntyres weren't big eaters by nature and necessity, but it had been just after sunup when he'd last had the eggs and some coffee with Mrs Grant. He needed his wits about him very badly and hunger was beginning to kick in and slow him down. Lizzie Grant hadn't known her pa would be following her out to the farm so she'd probably left his share of the stew at the forge. John Grant and Seb Reilly were big-made men and their hard physical work needed substantial meals. Kaid reckoned even Seb wouldn't be able to finish it off but, with Kaid's help, Lizzie would only have an empty pot to stack when she came back. No hurt feelings from thinking her pa's hired help had insulted her cooking skills and Lizzie sounded like she took offence very easily.

'Any luck, son?' The blacksmith rested the hammer on the anvil and wiped the sweat from his brow with an old red-checked neckerchief. 'Did you get whatever you came into Flat Stone for?'

Kaid shook his head and leaned against a tool-cluttered bench. 'Don't rightly know what I'm looking for.'

'The guy who beat up your pa, maybe,' suggested Seb.

'That's just it. All I wanted was a name, just a name. That simple and I thought there were enough folks in this rat-hole who'd love to point the finger. Big mistake.'

'The rats staying firmly holed up?' Seb knew Flat Stone's inhabitants only too well.

'Them that's emerged ain't squealing. Don't suppose you saw what happened?' Seb Reilly shook his head and sighed.

'Was over at that spread just off the Spike. Some wheels on one of their wagons bust and that, on top of the fact they hadn't bothered to keep the spares rust free, meant it was easier for me to go to them than the other way round. John was mad as hell but they coughed up the money — and it was some bill — on the spot, so he wasn't too put out this morning when I got back. Have you been asking the right folks?'

'Right folks, wrong answers. At least right folks by my reckoning, which might just be suspect.' Kaid was in a hopeless position and he was beginning to recognize it.

'You ain't got no judgement as to right or wrong, Kaid, for Flat Stone is a foreign land to you. It ain't your fault.' Seb Reilly had hit the nail squarely on the head, so to speak.

'Thought I'd have a word with the mountain men but Gertz got in the way.'

'The mountain men?' Seb thought that one through for a long moment. 'Could've been involved but I don't see why. Seems like your pa was after somebody — a score to settle. Mountain men settle theirs there and then so as there are no grudges borne from season to season.'

'Seems Pa was threatening one of

them with a knife.'

Seb Reilly smiled broadly, whilst shaking his head. 'Don't reckon that's so. You threaten one of them, you're dead meat on the spot.' But a look of puzzlement flitted across the blacksmith's face. 'All right, when did you say your pa came into town?'

'After dark.' Kaid was trying to think whether there had ever been any talk of mountain men in the past. But Seb was speaking again.

'Those hunters don't usually hang around that late. Loners, in a manner of speaking. They prefer the company of their own kind back at their campfire of an evening.'

'Well, one of them took a shine to Flat Stone,' said Kaid.

Seb put down the hammer. 'You hungry?' Kaid nodded and smiled ruefully. 'That the reason you came back here?'

'Kinda guessed the Grant girl had left grub for you and her pa and seeing as how her pa ain't here . . . '

Seb Reilly took the hint. 'John Grant's got some appetite so there'll be enough to feed a small army.' Seb whistled and a skinny lad appeared from out back. 'Watch the fire, son.' Seb replaced all the tools, washed in the water butt outside and Kaid followed him into the kitchen where Lizzie had left the pot simmering on a hook over the open fire. Seb swung the pot towards them and fetched a few tin bowls.

'Guess I can't be sure I'm asking the right questions but I'm certain I've asked the right people and got next to nowhere,' said Kaid.

'And you've no idea why your pa took off?'

'None.'

'Has to have been a very strong reason, son. This ain't Sunday.'

'I've only just found out what he did at Rattigan's every Sunday. Seems like he worked there.' Seb, Kaid knew, was a churchgoing man and never crossed Rattigan's threshold. Right then Kaid reckoned sourly that one of the drunks would have been of more use to him.

'And that surprised you?' Seb sawed through a loaf of freshly baked sourdough as he spoke.

'Sure did. Ma and me thought he was drinking every penny we had.'

'Never saw your pa with a drink in him.' There it was again.

'That's what surprised me.'

'That so?' Seb shook his head and his eyes narrowed as he ladled the thick stew into the bowls and then speared some potatoes alongside it, the aroma filling the room and telling Kaid Lizzie Grant was one helluva cook. The bread-knife sawed slowly through the sourdough once more as Seb cut a wedge, this time for himself. Both men sat at the table in silence, dipping the freshly baked bread into the gravy. Some time passed before Kaid spoke again.

'Seems all I'm doing is raising more questions than getting answers. I just don't know.' Kaid felt that he was suddenly climbing a mountain. Pa had worked in Rattigan's and yet money on the farm was in very short supply. Worked himself to death. So where did the money go? To pay a mortgage Kaid never even knew existed? One thing was certain, a man didn't get himself into the exhausted state Pa was in every Monday sunup for no reason at all. It made absolutely no sense to Kaid.

'Seems to me, Kaid, you should have come here armed with a few facts. Maybe it would be safer to go home and wait for Jerem to come to and set you straight.'

'He'll not come to soon, and possibly never, and I ain't got time to hang about.' Seb ladled some more potatoes and stew into their bowls. The extra gravy was soon soaked up by the sourdough and at last, both men sat back, well-fed at John Grant's expense. The strong, black coffee the blacksmith offered slid slowly down Kaid's throat as Seb cut himself another slice of sourdough and this time piled on the butter.

'So you've had words with the mountain men?'

'In a manner of speaking,' Kaid replied.

'Who else?'

'Walt Gertz. Don't reckon he'll be offering me a job.' Kaid smiled at the idea.

'You figuring on staying round long enough to want one?' Seb was shrewd all right.

Kaid half-laughed.

'I guess not.'

'What did that rat have to say?' Seb downed some of the thick, black coffee after liberally helping himself to sugar.

'Just that Pa had worked there. Things took a different turn then and if the mountain men hadn't spoken up, I'd have been flat out like Pa.'

'Speak to anybody else?'

'The preacher.'

'Oh, the Reverend Ben McWilliams. The man of God who, as the Good

Book says, helps 'justice roll down like a stream of water and honesty like a flowing tide' as long as he doesn't get his feet wet.' Seb, churchgoer or not, was not an admirer of the preacher.

'He was the one who saw Pa threaten the mountain man with a knife.' Seb bit into the buttered bread and chewed thoughtfully before speaking once more.

'That it?'

'Yeah, didn't see any more for he had to drive the buggy over to see the old lady at the Triple X who's real sick. He didn't get back till near sunup.'

'Some folks take a long time dying, it seems — no offence meant, son,' the blacksmith added hastily.

'None taken. So what next? That's what I've got to figure out. Who did see Pa? Did the mountain men lie in wait for him?' Kaid was bankrupt where feasible new ideas were concerned.

Seb shook his head. 'That makes no sense. Not their style with humans. They finish off quarrels there and then like I already said. You said your pa was looking for somebody. If that guy had been a mountain man, Jerem wouldn't have scared him away. Wouldn't have scared him period. My advice to you is to go back to the preacher and have another talk.'

'Says he wasn't in Flat Stone when Pa was beaten up.'

'Oh yes he was. That buggy was right here till he came for it this morning. Been back there being fixed since the day before yesterday. Like John said, we've been real busy this past week. Seems like the Reverend really ain't too hot on justice when it suits him.' Seb mopped up the gravy and settled back in his chair. Kaid watched absently and reckoned he'd walked right into a quagmire. Barring the Grants and Seb, it seemed to him the folks of Flat Stone Creek were all liars.

'Why did he lie to me?'

'That, Kaid, is what you're goin' over there to find out. Feel I should offer you a decent gun, son. Yours is a bit old, to put it mildly, and having to try to disentangle it from your trouser belt might just slow you down a bit.' The point wasn't lost on Kaid.

'Don't reckon I'll need one just talking to a preacher.'

Seb grinned on hearing that. 'You've been on the farm too long. Kind of tricky to judge whether wearing one's the right thing to do, though. Just strapping it on says to the trigger-happy boys you might just use it and they get their shot in first. But as you've already got one on you, I guess that decision's already been made. Remember, Kaid, farm boys ain't usually reckoned as worthy opponents, but anyone who beat up a quiet guy like your pa wants careful watching. Since you don't know who he was, you'd best treat everybody with extreme caution. You get me?'

'Yeah, Seb, but I guess I'll handle any trouble with these fists instead and leave Pa's old Navy Colt with you.' Kaid's hands were large and rough and brought a frown to Seb Reilly's brow as he was handed the gun.

'That's farmer talk, son. You won't be the one to decide when you'll need the gun and there ain't a guy in Flat Stone gonna wait till you go off to fetch it.' With that he raised the lid of an old oak chest the likes of which Kaid had never seen before.

Inside, he caught a glimpse of beautiful tanned brown leather, the leather of a holster whose lines spelled quality of the highest order, the product of a true craftsman, the finest money could buy. The legend 'JK', the maker's initials, was tooled into the leather and Kaid believed Seb when he said John Grant had waited six months for it to be made specially for him. A Peacemaker, its carved ivory handle showing, finished the set, the entire lot in pristine condition. This was no blacksmith's gear and Kaid looked up quickly at Seb. Seb shrugged and offered no further explanation. Kaid didn't press for one, for every man in the West was leaving something behind, it seemed, and all were entitled to their privacy. Give them it, for that was the best way to survive.

'You'd better decide right now, Kaid.'

Kaid shook his head. 'These fists will do the business. Thanks all the same.' He watched as the lid was replaced and hoped he'd made the right decision. The preacher was in it somewhere but he'd never seen him wear a gun. Never even had one in his buggy, according to what Ma had always said. Protected by a more potent force than a mere handgun, it seemed.

'They're here if you change your mind.'

Kaid moved away as the clean click of the chest's lock cleaved the silence in the room. There was no sound of a key being turned in it and Kaid was glad, for there was no way he wanted the opportunity totally barred to him. He was a farm boy all right, but there were no greater realists than those who worked the land. The merest nod of the head from that huge man left no doubt in Kaid's mind that his thoughts had been read and approved of. Kaid turned to leave. 'Be seeing you,' he called back.

Seb raised his hand in salute and watched till Kaid was some distance away before turning into the searing heat.

'Boy!' he yelled to the wiry kid by the bellows, 'when he comes back for the Peacemaker and if I ain't here, give it to him.'

'Think he'll need it?'

'I'm afraid so, son, and he'll need all the help we can give him.'

The long look wasn't lost on the boy. 'Can you spare me a minute, Seb?'

Seb nodded approvingly.

Kaid stepped out into the heat of the day but somehow felt cold. His eyes drifted along the road that snaked its way back out of Flat Stone before cutting across country to the lush foothills of the Sephina Mountains. It was a road he'd been planning on taking, a road that seemed forever just beyond his reach. But not any more, for freedom beckoned and it would be his in the next day or so. The day was wearing on and shadows were beginning to lengthen but Main Street was packed with cowboys, traders and mountain men now come down to the valley floor to trade their wares of the previous winter. Kaid made his way amongst sweating horses and noisy humanity and was aware that the shouts asking if his pa was dead had ceased. Flat Stone Creek knew something he didn't and right then, the chill he was feeling seeped straight into his very soul, somehow smothering the hatred of the human race that had always lurked there. Pa could live or die, it was of no matter to him. But there was something hidden here and Kaid wanted to know what it was. He wanted to know so badly now, could already feel the anger rising within him, that he was glad for the preacher's sake that he'd refused the gun.

Kaid could see that the bench where the reverend had been sitting was now empty. He reckoned the preacher might be in the meeting house, for his buggy was sitting out back, his horse under the shade of a lean-to just behind it. Kaid decided he'd head up the narrow alley running alongside and surprise the preacher. A mountain man had been threatened by Pa. The very notion of one of these hard-featured, self-sufficient men being scared off by Jerem McEntyre waving a knife was ludicrous. Kaid's thin blue shirt was streaked with sweat and years of wear and the ladies of Flat Stone knew what that meant in financial terms. They knew exactly whom to avoid and that day they did just that as he slowly made his way round to the alley. Everything about him shouted 'loser'. And Kaid McEntyre, if he'd been aware of it, would have approved of their decision. He'd seen the dire consequences of women tied to such men, women too poor and too loyal to walk away.

His boots crunched on the dusty pebbled ground as he moved alongside the meeting house, the buggy some way off to the right where the alley opened out. There was an odd stillness back there as if a shutter had been pulled down, slicing off the sounds of humanity, leaving only a void, a void now filled by the ferocious thundering of hoofs as suddenly a rider and horse thrust themselves into the emptiness before Kaid, bearing down like a vision of death to trample him into the dust. 'Ashes to ashes, dust to dust', he heard the preacher intone somewhere in his mind as he received a blow from a bullwhip across the brow of his head. The sheer glancing weight of the horse slammed him into the side of the building as it stormed past and Kaid McEntyre's slim body catapulted off the clapboard and into the eternal red dust.

Pain and blackness engulfed him, for how long he didn't know, but when he came to all was still in the alley and his head and body hurt like hell. He tried to sit upright, to think straight, to get himself to safety, but it was no use. He slumped back on to the hard ground and began to crawl back against the wall. He'd make for the stable round the back. It would be cool and there would be water for the horse — water he'd use to clear his head. He'd rest there a while, size up what damage had been done and then take it from there.

No sense in seeing the preacher. The Reverend McWilliams was running scared. Kaid wished to God Lizzie Grant was around. She'd know how to fix anything that was broken with no fuss and no questions — not till later anyway. But once again the blackness overtook the searing pain in his head and body and he knew he'd just have to lie there till it subsided.

'Get up, mister!' Kaid's body was being shaken and the new sharp pain cleared his brain of the blackness.

'You'll have to help me, kid.' There was no way Kaid could do it by himself.

'Think your legs still work?' The

blacksmith's errand boy looked doubtful as he asked his question.

'Yeah. Let me lean on you.'

'Where do you figure on goin'?' The boy took Kaid's weight.

'The preacher's stable.'

The boy shook his head. 'That ain't a good idea,' he advised. 'In fact it's a very bad one, mister.'

'Why?' Kaid just wanted to lie down — for ever.

'They've just found the preacher out back. Dead!'

That cleared Kaid's head double-quick.

'What? Dead?'

'Yeah, dead as in he ain't gonna preach no more this side of the Great Divide. Seems he fell down the well as he went to fetch water for his horse.' That changed everything. The boy waited for Kaid's sluggish mind to work.

'OK. The Grants' place.'

'Fine, but you'd better move yourself, mister, move yourself real fast and we'll go round the back alleys.'

Kaid was now on his feet, leaning heavily on the blacksmith's helper. 'Ain't possible right now.' Every bone and muscle in McEntyre's body screamed to be left alone.

'It'll have to be because I know something the sheriff doesn't, but he will as soon as the reverend's wife gets here.'

'And what's that?'

'The reverend never fetched water from that well. That's my job and there's enough water for the time being. I always check about now. The reverend knew that and so does his wife. My guess is somebody must have tipped him over the wall and you're the only one by the meeting house who looks like he's been in a brawl.'

'Fast as you like, kid. Let's go.'

4

It took only a few minutes to reach the blacksmith's but it felt like hours as Kaid's brain lurched about inside his head producing agony with every dragging step. But the kid bore the brunt of his weight without flinching. The blood from Kaid's head wound hadn't ceased flowing and it trickled down into his eyes, only the sound of hammering and a sudden searing heat telling him they'd reached safety.

Kaid crashed down on to one of the old threadbare chairs that served the blacksmiths on their breaks, grateful for its support and the lessening of the piercing pain shooting through his bruised body. The boy's medical aid was primitive, for suddenly McEntyre's head was hauled up by the fair hair and plunged momentarily into a bucket of ice-cold water. It worked as far as clearing out the blood from his eyes but failed miserably to stop the blinding pain in his head. A rough cloth was thrust into his hands as he sat back upon the chair and the silence about him told him he was now alone in the back room of the forge.

His eyes slowly focused on his surroundings as he took a mental note of the state of every part of his wiry frame. He breathed deeply and was relieved to realize that nothing appeared to be broken, all ribs intact, it seemed. Kaid heard someone come into the room behind him.

'Probably only bad bruising and a head like the hammers of hell are doing overtime in there?' Seb Reilly's voice held a note of amusement.

'Right.'

The blacksmith grinned as Kaid confirmed his own diagnosis. 'Just luck, son, and the boy being right on your tail.'

'And that was no accident, was it? Couldn't have been or he wouldn't have appeared so fast in that alley.'

'The boy would have to answer that. That kid's a law unto himself.' There was a kind of pride as well as a smile in the blacksmith's voice.

'Thank God for that,' said Kaid with feeling.

'Here!' The boy himself suddenly appeared, thrust a mug of milky coffee into Kaid's hand and gave another large one, of a distinctly treacly black appearance to the blacksmith. 'You have to stay real quiet with a head like that.' The boy took a long draught of cool, clear water himself as he spoke. Kaid suppressed a smile and thanked Providence for the boy's curiosity and interest in healing. There was silence for a time, all three lost in their own thoughts and Kaid was surprised how the creamy, sweet-tasting liquid supplied a permeating comfort if nothing else. He looked long and hard at the boy squatting on the floor opposite him.

'What's your name?' Kaid reckoned

his unknown saviour had a right to be called by his given name.

'You didn't need to know it back in that alley.' This surly answer was met with a shrug from McEntyre.

'Point taken.' The boy had a right to privacy, too, if that's what he wanted.

'He's just a nosy sonofabitch who sprang out of nowhere and Ellie Grant took him in,' said Seb Reilly, eyeing the boy with approval. 'Does as he bloody well pleases.' Grudging admiration was given and a slight smile from the boy betrayed his pleasure at the compliment.

'I know what I'm worth.'

'Right now you ain't worth nothing because you ain't doing nothing.' Seb was a realist.

'I ain't working for Mr Grant right now.' The boy finished his drink with a loud gulp.

'But you're mighty free with his coffee.'

The boy ignored the last comment. 'I'm working for Mr McEntyre there.'

'I don't need any hired help. Couldn't afford it even if I did.'

'See to the bellows! Get blowing!' Seb's cup clattered off the table as he spoke. The boy reluctantly made his way out of the room, for work meant money for food, and food was what kept body and soul together. Kaid and the blacksmith both smiled as he left and Kaid tossed one of the few coins he had on him on to the table.

'See he gets it, Seb.'

'Yeah, but as soon as you're thinking straight, I'll send him back through and you can find out what he saw. He's a clever kid, sees everything, says little. Makes his own mind up who he helps.'

'Guess he likes losers, then?'

'Nope. Lizzie Grant doesn't like you and that's a good enough recommendation for him.'

'Those two fight?'

'Like cat and dog. Bouts are about even so far. You rest up till he comes back through here.'

Kaid lay against the back of the

threadbare chair, exhausted, and wished the searing pain behind his eyes would ease off. His thoughts were abruptly shattered as the coin clattered into the wooden bowl on the pine stool by the chair.

'I don't charge innocent victims for help!' The boy's anger was almost tangible.

'Glad to know it.' Kaid put the coin back into his pocket without arguing. Seemed like that kid had more money than he had. His thoughts were now totally focused.

The boy took what seemed to be his customary seat on the floor, legs crossed, eyes steady on Kaid's face. He shrugged again, anticipating Kaid's question.

'I know nothing.' He watched McEntyre's reaction.

'Then tell me everything you know nothing about.'

The boy grinned at Kaid's words. 'The drink — the coffee, milk and sugar?' It was a question the boy somehow wanted answered first.

'Sure helped.' The usual bitter coffee would have exaggerated the pain but the boy's concoction hadn't. The boy's steady gaze held Kaid's until he was satisfied he was being told the truth.

'Like I said, mister, I know nothing.' And Kaid accepted that as the truth. 'But I'll give you a few guesses.'

'That's fair enough.' This kid was nobody's fool and Kaid reckoned he'd get exactly what the boy knew or thought was important and nothing else.

'Saw your pa after he'd got hurt real bad. Helped him back to your farm.' Shocked silence emanated from Kaid McEntyre, his mind and his power of speech divorced momentarily. He hadn't expected this.

'You brought him back to the farm?' Kaid's eyes searched the boy's face fearing the accusation he knew was coming.

'Should've been you, his son, not me, a stranger.' The accusation exploded all of Kaid McEntyre's self-pity and left him feeling the empty, worthless human being this boy had rightly labelled him. Kaid closed his eyes as shame washed over him, closed his eyes so as not to see the contempt in the kid's face. 'I knew your pa from Rattigan's. I help out there now and then, so he trusted me when I found him lying halfway along the trail.'

Kaid couldn't believe it but forced himself to go on, to appear in control. 'So what was a kid your age doing out there at that time of night?' Anything he could think of to avoid the obvious comment the boy was hell-bent on making.

'Looking for your pa like I'd have looked for my own if he hadn't come home and it gone two in the morning.'

'So how did you know he'd be there?'

'I knew where he was supposed to be. Whole town knew where he'd already been hammered and were avoiding it. He wanted everybody to know where he'd be that night — right out back of the meeting house. Nobody, but nobody, wanted to be the one to find the body.'

'So they all expected somebody to kill my pa?'

'Yeah, like I said, we all knew he was forcing a showdown and that he'd no chance of walking away from it. Nobody wanted to be anywhere near it. Not their fight.'

'But you ain't Mr Nobody, right?'

'Right. I went to cover him up.'

'But he wasn't dead like he was supposed to be?'

'He wasn't there at all. We were all working late, me and Mr Grant, and I couldn't get away. Mr Grant said it would all come to nothing as your pa wouldn't do anything foolish while he still had you to look out for. I just had to make sure. Well, I know your pa. Talked now and then over back of Rattigan's of a Sunday. Knew he'd try to make it back to his boy if he'd got hurt.'

Kaid stood up abruptly and every bone screamed at the effort. 'Back to you,' the kid emphasized, 'back to his boy.' The kid looked long and hard at Kaid as he uncrossed his legs and stood up. His voice softened, his piece had been said. 'You should go home, too, and rest up a little. You're in no fit state to come out of this in one piece. It can wait.'

Kaid looked at him. This was just a kid who was better equipped to survive in Flat Stone than he himself was. Kaid bit back an angry, embarrassed retort.

'Who was riding the horse — in the alley?' His voice and emotions were now well under control.

'I didn't see it. As I was going round to the back of the meeting house — well, I didn't want you to know what I was up to — old man Sleigh stopped me to ask me to help out over at his spread next week, and by the time I'd caught you up it was all over. I came round the back as they disappeared and one horse's tail looks much like another's, but I can tell you who wasn't where he should've been the night Mr

McEntyre was beaten up and left for dead. But not till you've rested up and are truly fit to act on my information. It'll keep.'

The boy was right and Kaid knew it.

'They're not gonna let up on you so you'd best beat it back to the farm and let Mr Grant and Lizzie keep an eye out for you. That Lizzie's something else with a rifle and she took one with her in the buggy.'

'Guess I've got my work cut out to find out what it's all about.'

'Flat Stone's a real sick town, mister, take my word for it, and there's only the liberal use of the knife will cure it. I've saddled the horse for you.'

'I guess you're right.' At that moment, Kaid wasn't physically ready to take on anybody and the boy had just proved his brain wasn't sharp enough either. 'Tell me this. Did you and my pa ever talk — I mean more than just the time of day?'

'Only rarely, now and again. But he watched out for me just the same. Till I could handle myself, that is, and then nothing.'

Kaid nodded as he eased himself from the old chair. 'He was never much on conversation.'

'Might've been once. Too dead inside now to bother, I reckon. That laugh of his always set me off too, though, in the old days when I was just a kid. You as well, I suppose.'

What laugh? What was there ever to laugh about? Kaid turned away and made for the forge and was relieved to see that the boy had taken the affirmative for granted.

'Seems some guys passed Pa lying hurt on the trail.'

'Yeah, I saw them. Ranch hands. I hid while they rode on by. Your pa was about a mile ahead of me then. But, like I said, it'll keep.'

Kaid nodded and sought out the blacksmith in the workshop.

'I'll be on my way, Seb.' But Gorman, it seemed, had other ideas.

'Oh no you won't — at least only as

far as the jailhouse.' Kaid's way was blocked by Sheriff Gorman and his men, strung along and barring his exit. Gorman's words were followed up by an obvious attempt at seizing Kaid but the massive form that was the blacksmith suddenly made his move.

'Out! This is private property, Gorman, so you'd better explain yourself and have it backed up by some paperwork before this rifle goes off and takes somebody's head with it — yours, probably, since you're nearest. Now back off — out into the street.'

'Easy, Seb, easy there. No need for firearms. Just want to talk to McEntyre here about the reverend — the late reverend.'

With that Gorman turned back to Kaid, his expression showing no obvious surprise at the cuts and severe bruising about Kaid's face and head. The kid had hit it on the nail. There was no way he was in any shape to take on the wolves baying for McEntyre blood in Flat Stone Creek. 'You were seen talking to the preacher and now he's dead.'

'I was seen talking to you and you're not — yet.' It crossed Kaid's weary brain that he was wasting his time. He should've moved out of Flat Stone long since. Should have crawled back home like his pa.

'Difference is passers-by heard you threaten him and next thing he's pulled out of the meeting house well dead.'

'Cause of death, drowning. He won't be the first man to topple in.'

'Nor the last — I agree with you on that, but he toppled in with a knife in his heart and it looks mighty like the one your pa was waving about last night. Now, we all know your pa's out of town and busy departing this life. And we also know the McEntyres use everything till it's falling to bits. They give nothing away so it stands to reason the only other McEntyre alive must've fallen heir to it. In other words, you. Did the preacher topple in before you had the chance to pull the blade out

100

again?' Kaid felt the net closing in on him.

'I never threatened the preacher and I ain't never carried a knife. There's no way you can prove I had one on me today.' Being economical with the truth was catching in Flat Stone.

'You're the only man known to have ever said a bad word about him. So what did you say to him?'

'Just asked him if he'd seen my pa last night.'

Gorman couldn't have cared less about any answer Kaid would give him. It was written all over his face. But he was willing to go through the motions just the same. 'And had he?'

'Yeah. Just round about Rattigan's as usual.' Kaid knew he was wasting his time.

'And?'

'And nothing,' said Kaid watching the deputies closely. Gorman's boys were getting restless and the sheriff moved closer to McEntyre as he spoke.

'You were seen heading for the

meeting house shortly before Reverend McWilliams was found dead and it looks like you've been in a fight.'

'Never reached it. Got in the way of a horse. Blacked out for a bit. Who found him in the well?'

'The boy here.'

Kaid's eyes pierced right into the boy's very soul, it seemed, but he never flinched. Gorman waited for the boy to speak and he duly obliged.

'I went to see if the bucket for the reverend's horse needed topping up like I always do about then and saw the blood on the side of the well. I looked into it and saw him. I reckoned as the deputy was right opposite, it was my duty to let the lawmen take over. Didn't hang around as I can't stand the sight of blood.' The boy tried his best to look squeamish.

'Helpful kid, eh?' The sarcasm in Kaid's voice made the boy lower his eyes and Kaid felt trapped. Only Seb Reilly seemed prepared to hold out for the truth.

'Go on, tell everything you know.'

'I've just done that. I've been brought up to tell the truth and the reverend was always fair to me, Mr Reilly.' The kid had now established himself as honesty personified.

'Well, I guess that's it,' said Gorman, grinning. 'Unless you know anything else, son?' The case was closed as far as the sheriff was concerned and Kaid's fate sealed, to the obvious delight of the deputies.

'No, sir, except I don't see how as McEntyre's the one that killed the preacher for as I came past the meeting house earlier, the Reverend McWilliams was shaking hands friendly-like with McEntyre here. Then he went in through the meeting house door and McEntyre walked off casual-like. I saw to the preacher's horse's feed and by the time I was finished, the reverend was reading the Good Book on his bench again, like always, and McEntyre looked like he was heading for Ratti-gan's. I know he went in there because

Carey Edmunds came running by minutes later shouting that Kaid McEntyre was fixing to get himself killed in the saloon. Don't seem to me there was any bad feeling there at all, no sir.'

'McEntyre came straight here once he'd left Rattigan's,' said Seb, his eyes firmly fixed on Gorman. 'At least ten guys could swear to that. There's a clear view straight from here to the saloon.' The blacksmith's finger hadn't relaxed on the trigger for one moment.

'And when you left here?' Gorman wasn't about to let go. Kaid knew it was going to sound bad that he'd intended confronting the preacher.

'I went to speak to . . . '

'To me. I'd just left the deputy when McEntyre here came over and said he'd help me drag some firewood round as payment for the hospitality shown his pa by the Grants. Being just a farm boy, he was used to that kind of labouring. That's the kind of folk these farmers are, skinny but strong.' That kid was some liar. 'He was walking ahead of me when a horse and rider came galloping past and McEntyre here just got in the way. Guess he ain't used to busy streets, him being raised on a farm. All happened too fast for me to recognize who it was.'

'Satisfied, Sheriff?' Kaid looked long and hard at Gorman.

'You're lucky Jude here saved your hide. I'll be back.' Gorman's disappointment could almost be tasted.

That at least gave Kaid McEntyre some degree of satisfaction. 'Guess that's the book closed on the reverend's death since I ain't guilty.'

'Resources are stretched in town right now what with all the traders and the like coming in. If you want to investigate, McEntyre, you go ahead.' That was exactly what Gorman wanted: Kaid McEntyre prowling around asking questions that would very definitely get him killed. There was somebody in that town with a definite aversion to questions or, more accurately, to the folks asking them.

'Got the feeling you could put your hand on the killer if you set your mind to it, Gorman. Guess the knife is being held as evidence.'

'You can have it back anytime you want,' said Gorman sarcastically. 'It's in the office. Look forward to a visit from you.'

'You'll get your visit, you can bet on that, but it won't be about any knife.'

Seb Reilly stepped forward as the sheriff and the others walked out into the dying light of the day. 'I'm shutting up shop, Kaid. You'd better ride like hell before the last of the daylight fades. And take the Peacemaker.' But the boy had anticipated that and the holster and Peacemaker were in Kaid's hands within seconds. McEntyre made the necessary adjustment and felt the unfamiliar weight of it all on his hips.

'You're some liar — Jude.'

'I've never lied in my life.'

'Shaking hands? Offering to help out? Don't remember that?' The boy just shook his head slowly and his look as he spoke held more than a passing resemblance to Lizzie's exasperated glance. 'So you found the preacher then beat it over to the deputy.'

'When I found you flat out in the alley, I shot off to get some water to bring you round. That's when I found the Reverend McWilliams. One of Gorman's deputies was heading in your direction, for that business with the horse was no accident. So I just diverted him by telling him about the preacher in the well, that's all, to give us a bit of time to get here. Knew nothing about any knife, for he was head down in the well when I saw him. I reckoned Seb wouldn't let Gorman take you. Like I said, the preacher was always fair to me, so the least I can do is find out what it was all about. I reckon you're a better bet to do that than Gorman. Set his widow's mind at case.'

'And you want me free to do that?'

'Yeah, and help your pa rest easy.'

Kaid's outstretched hand was taken and firmly shaken.

'OK. You got a deal. I expect in the long run we might manage to set the lady's mind at rest,' said Kaid, sounding more confident than he felt. Ride like hell was a fair piece of advice and Kaid aimed to take it, weary or not, head splitting or not.

'You ever gunned a man down before?' Seb was obviously concerned for a farm boy who was getting in way out of his depth.

'Nope, and I ain't ever stuck a knife in one either.'

'How come it was your pa's knife?'

'Says who?'

'Says Gorman.'

'My pa's knife's right by our cabin. Clean as a whistle like he always kept it. What that sheriff's got, any number of witnesses will swear it's Pa's. The McEntyres are too poor to knife somebody and leave the knife in him like he suggested. Don't make economic sense.'

'It would if the preacher toppled in unexpectedly.'

'Ain't possible, Mr Reilly.' Jude was once more the fount of all knowledge. 'Wall's too high. The preacher built it that high to keep that fool Edwin from tossing his ma's pies in when he was a young'un. Wastin' food was something the reverend was very sore on. That man was deliberately stuffed down it.' Jude's contribution finished the speculation yet again, and the 'why' would have to wait.

'You should aim to spend a couple of days getting your head fixed, Kaid,' said Seb, concerned at the head wound he'd sustained. 'Mrs Grant'll see to it.'

Kaid nodded in agreement and felt the pain surge yet again. 'I'll spend the night at the farm and be back here by noon tomorrow at the latest. Got a few things to sort out.'

'Ride easy and keep your wits about you.' Good advice from Seb and Kaid had every intention of taking it. He mounted up and wheeled his horse back into the side streets as Seb closed up the premises. If the sheriff had left someone on watch, he'd almost certainly be paying scant attention, the state of Kaid's head convincing everyone who'd seen him that he was in no fit state to go anywhere.

The full moon was starting to climb as Kaid eventually emerged from behind the last of the straggling buildings on the outskirts of Flat Stone and set out along the trail that skirted the McEntyre homestead, some four miles along the Decault Road and one mile north of the trail. The air was chill and bit into his still-throbbing head, the unseasonable heat having given way to a raw clear night. But there was still some fitful light as darkness was reluctant to fall completely. Kaid's senses were alert, heightened by the danger both he and his pa were now inexorably involved in. The harsh moonlight fitfully illuminated the trail and then plunged it into semidarkness as the moon drifted behind the slow-moving clouds.

'Buffalo Gal won't you come out tonight and dance by the light of the Moon?' That song from a long-forgotten childhood bounced around in his head unbidden and he suddenly wondered when they'd all stopped singing. His mind was scrambled now right enough. For the first time that day he doubted whether he was capable of taking on Flat Stone by himself and, if not winning, at least surviving long enough to feel Ma and the children would have been proud of him. Kaid felt dog-tired, the chestnut sorrel trotting softly and evenly along of its own free will. The constant contrast between moonlight and deep shadows played havoc with eyes already victims of the searing pain that once again was shooting through them. He suddenly sat bolt upright in the saddle as a deep voice echoed on the still night air.

'Just keep right on coming.' A brilliant burst of white moonlight lit up Kaid and wrapped the rider just ahead in silhouette. 'And don't even think of goin' for that six-gun. This rifle will blow your head right back to Flat Stone before that gun has cleared that fancy holster.'

'Nothing was further from my mind, mister,' Kaid managed to call out, despite the sudden shock. The rider came slowly on as the moon sailed yet again behind a cloud and Kaid recognized the youngest mountain man as he drew close, yet still far enough away to avoid being blood-spattered should Kaid prove Lizzie Grant right.

'You got company — just off to your right. Two of them, but they're no longer in any state to contribute to Flat Stone's deplorable record for unsolved crime.' Kaid's head turned involuntarily to his right at the mountain man's words. Was he the one who'd been threatened by Pa? Had Pa taken his hunting knife from him? That very idea was ludicrous and Kaid was once more aware of how vulnerable he was, both mentally and physically.

'Thanks.'

'Hate being interrupted, that's all.'

'Interrupted doing what?' Kaid didn't really want to know and, in spite of himself, he wondered if the men were now still alive. The hunter's voice had been flat, no intonation, no indication of feeling.

'Giving advice to you and I expect you to take it or I might just as well pull this trigger right now.' There was no doubt at all in Kaid's mind that it would take very little to swing the decision one way or the other.

'You don't leave me much of a choice, do you?' Kaid's stomach was churning, his breath coming in short bursts.

'Put like that, no. Now I'll say my piece and ride.'

But Kaid quickly interrupted him. 'They say the preacher was killed with the knife my pa had last night.' What reaction that was supposed to get, Kaid himself didn't know. His words were quickly brushed aside.

'That don't interest me. Now you're beginning to waste my time.' But Kaid plunged on.

'My pa threatened a mountain man with a knife. I reckon that might have been you, mister.' The rifle trained on him never wavered for a moment.

'Says who?'

'The preacher. The late Reverend McWilliams.'

'The late Reverend McWilliams? Well, that's one bit of information he ain't likely to repeat.'

'Why did Pa do it? He wasn't a fighting man. Why'd he do it? Why did he threaten you?' The mountain man's face remained expressionless, his entire body still, it seemed. Suddenly he clicked his horse into action and slowly circled Kaid and his horse.

'Like I said, I'm here to offer you advice. So here it is. Keep your mouth shut and keep riding right on past the dirt farm and don't ever look back.'

'My pa's a peace-loving man.' Kaid faltered as the rifle was aimed straight at his head and for a moment the night air seemed heavy with the hatred emanating from the hunter. Kaid forced himself to keep on staring at this unknown man, forced his every instinct down that called for making a break for it before the inevitable click of the trigger blasted him into eternity. There would be nobody to bury what was left of him on the rise beside the others.

'Nothing's gonna stop me finding out what this is all about. The McEntyres ain't all dead yet and I ain't quitting. Pa turned like the worm he'd been for fifteen years, but I ain't a worm and I'll finish what my pa started.'

'Your pa's evil — every bit of his body is riddled with it and I aim to put an end to it. I'll help him gather with the other saints by the beautiful river, as the late unlamented preacher would have said. Now don't you get in my way. I've no quarrel with you.'

With that, the mountain man rode off back along the trail but it was some minutes before Kaid McEntyre's breathing returned to normal. He intended killing Pa! Why? What had he done that was so evil a man would come all the way from the Sephina Mountains to put him in his grave? Kaid set off briskly for the farm and hoped to God his pa was able to talk and tell him what they were up against. Kaid knew his arrival at that time of night and in that physical state would probably scare the living daylights out of the Grants, but there was no way Kaid was going to ride right on by. There were questions that needed to be asked and answers needed to be given.

5

Kaid McEntyre felt the full force of the grit-filled dust right in his face and knew the wind would blow all day long. It always did, for there was nothing to stop it carving its way through the property.

'You aim to lie there all day whilst folks as good as strangers to you work your land and care for your livestock?'

Kaid smiled in spite of everything. A few hens and chickens hardly amounted to much. He realized too, that the dust he was chewing had hit him as a result of Lizzie Grant's boot kicking it in his direction. The wind was no more than a gentle breeze.

'Morning to you too, Lizzie.' Kaid hauled himself off the bench outside the cabin and felt exactly which parts of his body had smashed into the meeting house wall.

'You should've come inside last night. It's your house.'

The smile left Kaid's face as he slowly walked over to the water trough. Yesterday morning it had all been so clear. Pa gone at last and Kaid now free to move on. Yeah, the cabin was his all right — when Pa died — and he knew he'd torch it the minute he'd shovelled the last grain of red dust over him. He was aware of Lizzie Grant's gaze as he plunged his head into the chilly water and kept a firm grasp on his ability to swear as it revived the pain behind his eyes of the previous day.

'Like to watch the sun come up.' He could feel its rays beginning to burn even this early in the morning. He hadn't checked on Pa, reckoned if the sassy Lizzie was still here, her ma must still be trying her best. He knew the bruising on his own body and face had been noted but Lizzie still made no comment on it.

'Ma's making breakfast and Pa's seeing to the horses — all of them,' she added pointedly. Kaid got the message but his conscience was clear regarding Ellie Grant's horse — at least for the previous night. Those old habits again, for no matter how ill a man felt, he had to first see to his livestock.

'Real nice of him — of all of you,' he added quickly. She tossed him the apron she'd been carrying the corn in and he dried himself with it whilst scanning the horizon. 'Appeared an hour ago,' said Lizzie. They both watched the horsemen pace slowly back and forth some way off.

'You sure rise early,' he said for it was no more than just past sunup.

Lizzie ignored him. 'Four of them. Just sitting there. My pa says they're strangers.' Everybody who ever passed through Flat Stone called in at her pa's place and John Grant had a memory second to none. The riders the mountain man had sorted out had obviously been replaced. Kaid guessed they were either dead or temporarily incapacitated.

'Let them watch. I ain't going nowhere just yet.'

'And when you do go, I'm going with you.' John Grant had come up behind them and now stood beside Kaid.

'They're just watching. It don't mean nothing.' Kaid was returning to Flat Stone and he didn't need an escort. But there was no need to upset the Grants right then and no need to put them in any more danger. 'How's Pa?'

'Still breathing but that's about all. Come and eat. Better get that shirt on or Mrs Grant'll have you stinking of horse liniment, too. Or at least it smells like it.' Kaid quickly dressed and handed the wet apron back to the sullen Lizzie.

'What happened to you in Flat Stone?' At last she commented on the bruising and her eyes met his as he walked past her.

'Got in the way of a horse.'

'Hard to see, ain't they?'

Kaid kept right on going, for he was hungry and he needed to talk to his pa.

Lizzie Grant wanted to know what had happened and why, for somehow, Kaid knew, she reckoned she could suggest a solution. He had the feeling Lizzie was never short of solutions.

Suddenly he turned and faced her. 'How come you know my pa's smart?' But Lizzie had already dismissed Kaid from her mind as a bungling simpleton not worthy of an answer and was giving her undivided attention to the more intelligent hens.

Jerem McEntyre lay on the bed and looked as if all the life in him had been systematically drained away. Kaid looked at him closely for the first time in years and saw the hated figure as now no more than a crushed, near-lifeless form. He'd truly taken one helluva beating and Kaid could sympathize only now with the pain that that entailed, for at no time had beatings ever happened on the homestead. At no time had physical pain been part of their lives. It was a weariness of body and spirit that had worn them all down.

'He's much the same.' Mrs Grant motioned Kaid back out into the kitchen but Kaid didn't move, for he knew the man on the bed better than anybody. Or so he'd thought. Now he hesitated, no longer trusting his own judgement. 'He's miles away — in his mind. Might never come back, son, and you've got to prepare yourself for that. If he makes it at all.' Kaid still stood over the broken body.

'Who were you searching for?' Jerem McEntyre's eyes slowly moved from staring blindly into the middle distance and came to rest on Kaid's face. Those eyes were filled with such hatred that Kaid felt the hairs stand on the back of his neck. He wanted to lash out at him but held his temper in check. Somewhere along this trail he was now riding lay revenge, not for, but against this man, and he felt sure that when he tasted it, he'd feel clean at last. He turned abruptly but stopped by the door, for he wanted this evil person, for that was indeed what he was, to know and see the hatred he too felt in return. Their eyes met and the older man's never flinched till suddenly, from their pale depths, Kaid watched as a plea filtered through the hatred, a plea for his help in ridding him of it. Against everything he felt, Kaid was drawn back to the bed. He knelt down beside the supine figure and from somewhere in the distant past came a spark of understanding.

'Who, Pa, who do you hate so much? I can't do anything to help you unless you tell me. Is it the mountain man?' But Jerem McEntyre lapsed back into unconsciousness and Kaid suddenly felt at one with his pa and couldn't understand what was happening to him.

'That beating knocked him senseless.' Kaid slowly stood up as Mrs Grant spoke whilst she swept his pa's hair back off his forehead with an oddly tender touch of her large hand before quietly leaving the room.

'No, there ain't nothing wrong with

his brain, Mrs Grant,' Kaid called softly after her. He had to think, had to talk to Lizzie.

'Your pa's sleeping again, son?' The blacksmith spoke from the doorway.

'That he is, Mr Grant. Sure am grateful for all you folks have done for him. He'd have been a goner left to me. Ain't never nursed anybody who's had a beating.'

'Come on back through to the kitchen.' Kaid followed him and saw that the others were now all there.

'Sit down and eat and then I'll fix that head of yours,' said Mrs Grant, her eyes narrowing at the sight.

'He walked into a horse.' Lizzie's sassy tone broke the silence after John Grant had thanked the Lord for the food that they were about to eat. Kaid silently thanked Ellie Grant.

'Think it best you should rest up, too, Kaid. Looks like that horse must've been travelling at some speed.'

'I just came out to see Pa. Have a word with him.'

Ellie Grant shook her head knowingly. 'He's taken a blow to the throat. Too bruised for the time being to utter even one word. Even writing's beyond him. It'll all come back but right now he's too weak. You'll just have to wait, son.'

'I ain't got time for that, ma'am. There are too many people trying to wipe out the McEntyres.'

John Grant passed round the scones before speaking. 'Well, I've sent word to Seb to shut up the business and come on out here. And one to the sheriff saying I got permission from your pa to put a bullet in anybody who comes on to his property I don't take a liking to.' This obvious lie concerning the farm brought a slight frown of disapproval from his wife.

'Maybe it would be safer for you to go back to town and take the womenfolk with you, Mr Grant. I sure don't want anything happening to folks who've been kind enough to help Pa and me out.'

'Nothing'll happen here, son. But back in Flat Stone — well — that's another matter.'

'There's one guy you should be real careful about. A mountain man. Young guy. Swore he's gonna kill Pa.'

'We'll sort it out, Seb and me. You eat up while I take a wander round the place.'

Kaid was only too happy to eat up and the sounds of women chatting and laughing quietly stirred memories of a past long dead. His eyes drifted yet again to the open door of the bedroom. There had been hatred in those eyes and a softness, too, that had taken the feet from Kaid. But there had been no evil. Jerem McEntyre had been a whole lot of things it seemed, but evil wasn't one of them. Kaid was beginning to realize that he knew nothing of the man he called 'Pa' but he sure as hell was going to find out and no mountain man was going to stop him. Pa was safe from him bothering him for a while for the mountain men were hunters all right, but not of human prey. There was no honour in finishing off an injured man. He spooned the sugar carelessly into the strong, black coffee and waited till Mrs Grant had gone outside to hang out the wet towels.

'Got talking back there in Flat Stone with that kid, Jude — the one who helps your pa, Lizzie.'

'Did you?' Lizzie eyed him with something vaguely approaching interest.

'Clever kid.'

'That so?' Lizzie was in no mood for light conversation.

'Thinks highly of you.'

'So?' Get to the point was what she meant.

'Thinks you're real smart.'

'Get to the point.' There, it was out as Lizzie leaned against the dresser, the habitual scowl fixed firmly on him.

'The point is, you said my pa was smart. I'd like to know how you reckon that's so. What did he say or do that separated him from . . . '

'From you?'

This time it was Kaid's turn to scowl but right then he needed the sour-faced girl's help and the easy smile reasserted itself once more. Besides, Kaid knew as well as she did that he'd been a singular failure at what little schooling he'd had. There was no hiding-place from Lizzie.

'All right, me.'

'You weren't that bad. Just the Grant girls were smarter. Ain't your fault.' Lizzie Grant had called a truce. 'Used to see you and your folks walk into Flat Stone every Sunday for the church service.'

'Don't reckon there'll be one this Sunday.'

'Why ever not?' Mrs Grant bustled in and scooped up his cup to wash it as she went by. 'Is the reverend sick?'

'Well, if he was, he ain't any more. He's dead. Murdered.' The cup bounced off the corner of the table and only Lizzie Grant's quick reflexes prevented his ma's best china from smashing on the floor.

'John! Come in here! Did you hear that? The Reverend McWilliams's been murdered. Who'd do such a thing to a man of the cloth?'

John Grant's face mirrored his disbelief. 'No right-minded person, that's for sure. Who does Gorman think did it, son?'

'Me. Well, not exactly, he just hoped he could pin it on me.'

'But murdered.' Mrs Grant slumped into the chair she'd vacated some minutes before. 'Coffee, Lizzie, strong and black.' Lizzie left the dresser and Kaid hoped he hadn't lost his chance to speak to her. 'Who'd murder a preacher? Why, he's been here nigh on twenty years — came right out here from around the Powder River — and never offended anybody.' Ellie Grant was bereft of ideas.

'Why did the sheriff think it was you, Kaid?' asked her husband.

'I'd spoken to the Reverend McWilliams earlier, Mr Grant, and he was found dead down the meeting house well some time later. You know how Gorman feels about Pa and me.'

'So he drowned?'

'Nope. Had a knife in his chest and Gorman said it was Pa's. He was probably dead before he hit the water. Pa's knife is in that tin box right by the stable. Double checked myself last night when I came back. Besides, knives are ten a penny and Gorman knows it. Gorman said some folks — unnamed naturally — had reported hearing me threatening the preacher. The whole business is about somebody wanting the McEntyres dead — both of us.'

'How did you prove it wasn't you that — well, you know?' Murdering a preacher was just one step too far for decent people even to contemplate.

'Didn't have to. That kid, Jude, who helps out at your place, swore he'd seen me elsewhere at the critical time. And he'd no reason to lie.'

'And had he seen you?'

'Nope.'

'Little liar right enough,' said Ellie

Grant but with very few signs of disapproval this time. 'Law-abiding folks don't live their lives making sure they've got witnesses to everything they do.' She sniffed a little righteously.

'Likes Lizzie, though. Reckons she's the smartest person in Flat Stone.' Kaid avoided looking at Lizzie as he spoke.

'He's probably right,' agreed her father. 'Too smart and quick-tongued for her own good, though. I'm figuring on sending her back to her grandma in Indiana.'

Lizzie's scowl became even more pronounced. 'I won't go, Pa.'

'You ain't being asked, girl. There ain't a family hereabouts you ain't riled one way or another and that ain't good for business. For such a smart ass, you got no common sense.' Kaid wisely kept his head down for he needed information from the much-maligned Lizzie and riling her was no way to get it. He maintained what he hoped was a non-committal look on his face should it be seen, and hoped for the best. But

Lizzie obviously acknowledged fair comment when she heard it.

'But Indiana, Pa!' There was an odd vulnerability in her voice and Kaid wondered how it sat with the scowl. He himself was no smart ass but he sure had plenty of common sense. The deep dents in the old wooden table now had his complete attention.

'But who'd want to kill the preacher, that's what I'd like to know?' murmured John Grant.

'Maybe Lizzie here can come up with something,' Kaid suggested. But Lizzie had already slipped out by the time Kaid looked up, the thought of exile in Indiana having overtaken her desire to wipe the intellectual floor with Kaid McEntyre.

'How did the reverend seem when you spoke to him, Kaid? Edgy? Troubled?'

'Nope. Seemed his usual self. Full of his own importance.'

'Why'd you go over there anyway?'

'It all seems to have something to do

with Rattigan's and I'm damned sure the reverend saw everything that went on there. Based most of his sermons on the comings and goings he saw from the meeting house window. I just asked him a question or two — friendly like, and got nowhere. He not only saw nothing, he wasn't even there. Had to go out of town on an errand of mercy. But it seems his memory was just like the sick old lady — both ceased to exist — the preacher's memory, though, only for as long as I was asking questions.'

'And you threatened him?'

'Just in a general way in case he was lying. Turning the screw a bit, that's all.' Kaid felt slight pangs of guilt.

'And was he?'

'Yeah, for it seems his buggy was in your back yard getting fixed and we all know the preacher ain't happy to be on horseback, even just riding along Main Street.'

'Wonder why he lied.'

'Wonder what he saw. Two questions I set off to ask him but by that time he was already down the well and I was being trampled by that horse.' There was silence between the two men, each one deep in thought.

'Can't say as how I can make any of this out.' The blacksmith shook his head in bewilderment.

'Well, when I left Mr McWilliams, he was alive and smart-talking as always.'

'Wouldn't doubt that for a minute, Kaid. So who's this mountain man?'

'A guy who told me he intended killing Pa and that I was to stay well out of it.'

'You could do that quite easily. No ties and you and Jerem have never seen eye to eye. There's nothing to stop you from moving on.'

'That's nonsense, John Grant, and you know it.' Ellie Grant's face had now lost its pallor, and, like all Grant women, it seemed, she liked to add her bit. 'Apple of his eye you were, Kaid, way back when you all first trundled up Main Street, which was no more than a few shacks, a store and the meeting house. I said it then it was a big mistake. Do you remember, John? No future in this farm, poorest of poor land, but Jerem's heart must have been set on it for I never heard any talk of quitting.' The usual harsh, angry words sprang to Kaid's lips but were never uttered, for his black-and-white view of Jerem McEntyre had somehow evaporated and in its place there was now a reluctance to judge until he finally knew the truth. A sudden pain shot through his eyes and brought with it an odd memory of laughter and singing and a pa who'd been his hero. Kaid abruptly killed it. *Apple of his eye.* Kaid recognized little of it and needed none of it.

'Mountain men ain't usually talkative. Keep themselves to themselves. This one a renegade?' The blacksmith frowned as he spoke.

'Seems so. Young guy. Was sitting with that group that always camps over at Big Bluff.'

'They're from the Sephinas, Pa.'

Lizzie was once more in the cabin and in a talkative mood. Kaid looked up at her as she spoke. 'Ma. You'd best give him something to keep his head clear. Pain'll dull his reactions, such as they are.'

'Thank you kindly,' said Kaid. His sardonic smile brought a fleeting look of annoyance to Lizzie's pale features. 'I'll be fine, Mrs Grant, just need some sun on my back and I'll be gone.'

'He'll need a gun, Pa. That one of Mr McEntyre's pulls to the right three times out of four, so he told Jude once. Where have you hidden it? Seb got it?' But Lizzie's question was answered by another from Kaid.

'When did he tell Jude?'

'Don't matter when, it just does.' Lizzie looked steadily at Kaid and he thought she could read every corner of his mind. 'I reckon he won't take yours, Pa, no matter what you say.' She left and Kaid wondered if she had the second sight.

'Now, son, you might not be much of

a shot but you should at least have a fighting chance. This one I've got here is perfectly good. The rifle will be more useful to me here on the farm. I don't reckon on letting any guy near enough for a handgun to be effective.'

'Mr Grant, I don't know who I'm up against and I don't expect to get a chance of any kind. Not his style if the reverend's fate's anything to go by.'

'That's foolish talk, son. You can't beat whoever's out there just by hope.'

The cabin door burst open and Lizzie reappeared. 'He's got no intentions of relying on hope, Pa, no intentions at all, for he's got your best Peacemaker and the JK holster that practically ejects the six-gun all on its own.' Lizzie tossed them to Kaid. 'Hid them under the bench he slept on last night, Pa. Seb Reilly gave you them, didn't he?'

Kaid nodded. 'Hope he did right, Mr Grant.'

'Seb Reilly's judgement is second to none. Glad he did.' The blacksmith nodded his approval as he spoke and this time saw his wife's agreement in her smile. But Lizzie Grant wasn't finished yet.

'Now, you see and give them back to my pa when it's all over.' But this time the girl's voice was soft as she spoke to Kaid and the reassuring smile transformed the scowling features and abrasive attitude. At least she reckoned there was a chance he might survive.

'For you, Lizzie Grant, anything.' Kaid's slow smile answered her own.

'We'll keep an eye out for the mountain man, son,' promised her father.

'Don't reckon he'll be around for a bit, Mr Grant, since Pa's still weak.'

'Hate robs a man of his judgement, Kaid, and his honour. He ain't likely to stick around more than a day or so for they've done their trading and they'll be heading back to the high country any time now. We'll stay close and Seb's due in an hour or two. He's just finishing off one or two jobs and then he'll come on out.'

'Your stew was real good, Lizzie.' Uttering compliments didn't come easily to Kaid and he hoped Lizzie appreciated the effort. 'We finished off what you'd left for your pa.' Lizzie's most potent look of contempt was reserved now for Kaid McEntyre alone.

'You were right, Pa. These Tennessee boys talk a lot of trash. Jude made the pot that was left over the fire and, as well as a liar, he's no good as a cook.' After a lifetime of the cheapest cuts liberally seasoned with red dust, Kaid reckoned he'd been fooled by the best meat money could buy in these parts.

'Then it's just as well you're destined to grace some Indiana guy's table. They sure know good cooking when they taste it, I'm told.' McEntyre relished the small victory that was his as Lizzie's eyes mirrored the anguish she felt.

'Pa, you ain't thinking along these lines, are you? Ma?' The door banged shut as Lizzie stormed out yet again to come to terms with her possible fate.

Kaid went slowly after her, leaving the Grants to speculate on why the reverend had been killed.

Lizzie was sitting on the bench that had served as a bed for Kaid the previous night. Kaid strapped on the holster and felt the weight of the Peacemaker against his thigh as he walked to her side.

'Don't look so down, Lizzie. Your pa's just fooling. Bet he and Seb have been talking about Indiana for weeks now in front of you.' Lizzie nodded and slowly wrote her initials in the red dust with a stick. 'And you sound off the minute they do.' She nodded again and the opinionated girl looked thoroughly miserable. 'There's no way they're going to lose having a bit of fun at your expense. They know you go off the deep end and that's exactly what they want. You're clever all right, Lizzie, but there's no fun in you.'

'And you're a laugh a minute, Kaid McEntyre.'

'Laugh hardly at all, I guess. You're

right, Lizzie, but for a different reason from you. I need to ask you something.'

'Go ahead.' Lizzie's eyes were watching the horizon.

'What did you mean when you said Pa was smart?'

She shrugged before answering. 'Clever. Interested in things and places beyond Flat Stone Creek. Talked about a world way beyond Flat Stone. About the books he'd read long ago.'

Kaid struggled to understand what she was saying. 'Places like Indiana?' Lizzie didn't rise to the bait and Kaid had to think fast, for she'd begun to move off. 'When did he talk to you about that kind of thing?'

'He didn't. He didn't talk to anybody — except Jude sometimes, like I said. Just worked — all the time, he just worked. I watched him getting driven into the dust. Saw it in his eyes. You said he threatened the mountain man. I can't believe he cared enough about anything any more to do that.' Lizzie turned suddenly and looked directly at him. 'What happened to make him hate enough to live just one last time? I reckon it must have been you. What did you say to him that day he went into town all fired up? He only ever cared about his family so what did you do to set him off that day? What does anybody say to make a man so willing to get himself killed?'

Kaid turned away from a gaze that was no longer curious but accusing. He knew the answer to that but at no point had he realized that Jerem McEntyre had given a damn about him or any of the others. But Lizzie had finished and was watching the riders on the horizon, now dismounted and seeking shelter for themselves and their mounts amongst the gnarled trees and sagebrush from a sun that was beginning to burn up everything it touched. Kaid rose and headed for the cabin.

'Be seein' you, Lizzie.'

'You take care, Kaid.'

He turned back to her once more and shook his head. 'Always were fond of dumb animals, the Grants.'

Lizzie smiled broadly and Kaid wondered fleetingly what Indiana was like.

He could smell the aroma of baking and signalled to the Grants as he passed through the kitchen that he was just going to have a last word with his pa.

'I'll bring the horse round, Kaid.' John Grant left and his wife found something which needed her immediate attention in the yard. Kaid knelt down beside the sick man, a deathly silence hovering about him. He gently touched the older man's hand, saw the anguish in those pain-filled eyes and felt the first stirrings of an emotion other than hate course through him in response to a look that said his pa cared for him. 'I don't know what this is all about, Pa. Maybe I'll come out of it wanting to kill you, maybe get myself killed doing it, but one way or another, I'm gonna find out why the singing stopped.'

6

Kaid was aware of the riders following him but knew they'd make no move to harm him without Gorman's nod. It was having the mountain man away to his right that spooked him. He'd appeared a mile or so back out of nowhere. Patience was a mountain man's byword. There was nothing he himself could do that the Grants hadn't already covered. He was tempted to stop and see whether he would come right on, but Kaid had no time to waste.

'You just gonna sit there all day?' he shouted over to the hunter as the chestnut sorrel moved steadily along. The man sat still as a statue in the saddle and Kaid realized that that was how he tracked his quarry. Had he been the one riding that horse out back of the meeting house? Not his way!

Kaid reined in his horse. 'You keep away from my pa or I'll track you down if it takes the rest of my life!'

The man never flinched and Kaid hoped the blacksmith was as good with a rifle as he was with a hammer. He heeled the horse into action once more and soon entered the outskirts of Flat Stone Creek, now very much aware of the gun and holster's weight against his right thigh. He was quick on the draw, he knew that. The only thing was he'd never drawn from a holster, and how accurate he was was an unknown factor, for bullets had been few and precious on the farm and that had left nothing to actually fire from his pa's old Navy Colt. He rated his chances in a set gunfight as zero, so that would have to be avoided at all costs.

'Your pa dead yet?' The same old question. Maybe it would all stop if they heard that he was.

'Just about.'

'Too late to come for the preacher, then, for they're burying him right now.

Got a preacher over from Gartville who was visiting some kinfolk to say the words.'

Kaid rode on and heard the singing off to his left. Somehow, he just couldn't ride on by. There'd be people hurting there, family and friends, and he dismounted out of respect at the foot of the rise a few hundred yards behind the meeting house. He looked back and watched as Gorman's men swung their mounts off in the direction of Rattigan's. Kaid McEntyre was in town and the sheriff would be mighty pleased to hear that. It was no more than minutes before the lawman appeared at his side.

'You set on being lynched, son?'

'You got a rope?'

'Could have.'

'Bet you had a helluva time burning witches.' Kaid was aware of Gorman's deputies on all sides.

'A bit before my time.'

'Can't win them all, Sheriff. But I guess a good hanging makes up for it

— or a good beating.'

'You're confusing me with your pa, son.'

'Seems everybody in Flat Stone's an expert on my pa except me.'

'So whose fault's that?' That hit the mark and Kaid felt his face flush as the sheriff leaned lazily against the gatepost of the bit of land marked out for the dead. That gatepost had been there ever since Kaid could remember and no-one had ever bothered to put up the gate that should have gone with it.

'That ain't the question you should be asking, Sheriff.'

'So what is?' Gorman was happy to humour him.

'Maybe just the one about who beat my pa near to death. I'll find out myself why, if that's beyond your ability.'

'Bad things happen in the dark all over the world. Decent folks are in their beds by midnight. Don't happen to them. If a man goes prowling around at that time, he's just asking for a bullet in the head.'

'My pa walked the Decault Road for more than fifteen years at night — week after week — and nothing ever happened to him. So why now?'

'Wasn't himself, that night.'

'Says who? You?'

Gorman shook his head. 'The whole town. I only spoke to your pa that time, like I said. After that, I had business elsewhere.'

'The bawdy houses. Crowd needing controlling in there these days, was that it?'

'Now, you show some respect for the preacher here. This ain't no pauper they're burying over there, so hush up. These folks are hurting real sore for their spiritual leader and, as he was your own minister, so should you be.'

'The Reverend McWilliams never said any words over any McEntyres and they were all members of his flock.'

'We all reckoned what took your kin might be catching. That being the case, folks had to stay away.'

'The whole town again, eh? What

about the Grants?'

'It's well known blacksmiths ain't got no brains, just brawn.'

'Was three years from the first to the last. Three years is a long time to have something that's catching.'

'Four if you count your pa.' Pa again.

'Starvation ain't catching, just weakens the resistance.' But Kaid became silent just the same. Only the Grants had always been there offering help and even if it was never accepted, they'd kept right on coming. 'My pa ain't gonna die, Sheriff, so you'd better start getting your story straight for when he's fit enough to ask questions.'

'And he'd better be prepared to answer a few.'

'Like what?' This was what Kaid had been waiting for — the reason Gorman and the posse had come out to the farm.

'Your pa was wild that night, prowling around and muttering, ready to kill any guy who got in his way. I reckoned I owed it to the town to find out what he was going on about.'

'In his way? So a guy who was dead on his feet most days held the whole of Flat Stone to ransom with a knife? Don't make me laugh, Gorman. You're out to kill my pa, legal or otherwise, and I'm gonna find out who's issuing you with the orders. And I ain't gonna do it with no knife! This Peacemaker's prepared to break it, not make it — the peace that is, so back off. A boy just off the farm's liable to get a bit jumpy and you make quite a big target.'

'You're just wastin' your time. This persecution's all in your mind. You and your pa have got a bit unhinged. Comes from losing all your kin and staying away from normal folks.'

'If you're normal, Sheriff, then God help us all.'

Gorman was taking orders from somebody and maybe Kaid should have been finding out the sheriff's movements that night, as well as the preacher's. But just then the tunes of the old familiar hymns washed over him, and the Bible readings were identical to the words Pa had said from memory every time a new cross was put up on their own rise. He fervently hoped he didn't have to say them over Pa, and surprised himself by the depths of that desire. 'How did you find out about Pa taking a beating?'

'I didn't. Just saw how bad it was when we called at your place yesterday. Some guys were talking about seeing your pa on the trail as they'd come into town in the early morning. I just called to ask him about threatening people.' That'll be right, thought Kaid sourly.

'With a posse?'

'Knew he was violent. Now don't you get shirty with me, boy. Your pa was in one fight that night, right around the meeting house. Still, it wasn't much of a fight, for the other guy pulled a gun and that calmed your pa.'

'Who was the guy?'

'A drifter, probably visiting one of the girls. Said your pa was watching for somebody and he just got in the way. A decent sort of guy, for if he hadn't been, your pa would have died on the spot. Said he only gave your pa a slap or two.'

'After he'd drawn his gun?'

'Yeah, the sight of it seemed to sober Jerem up, in a manner of speaking.'

'So who showed up and found Pa wasn't there as arranged?'

'How the hell would I know? If he showed at all, nobody knows. Folks come and go there all the time. It's a busy place.'

'You said it.' Both men had been speaking quietly and now stopped altogether as the Reverend McWilliams was laid to rest. In the total silence surrounding the graveyard, the clatter of earth and tiny stones was heard as daylight shone on the reverend for the last time. Kaid's eyes avoided the sight. It was all too familiar to him and he'd have walked away. Only good manners held him there whilst the preacher's family slowly walked back down towards the entrance. Too late,

Kaid remembered being accused of having a hand in the reverend's death. The preacher's daughter suddenly lunged towards Kaid, her nails slicing through both his cheeks before her brothers dragged her away. Not a sound had been uttered by the girl and she continued to weep silently as they led her back up Main Street.

'You'd best get that seen to.' Gorman's concern was met with a scathing look from Kaid.

'That was all your doing. You knew I'd nothing to do with that and I'll bet you know exactly who did it. Seems to me you're being paid twice to do the same job — turning a blind eye, once by the town and once by somebody big in these parts. But nobody's paying me to hold my tongue and I aim to find out why my pa is public enemy number one or, more accurately, public scapegoat number one. You'd better take my advice, Gorman, and have those riders watch you instead of me, because when I find out who's behind this and why,

I'll be paying you a visit and you'll need all the help you can get. You're in this up to your neck, and I'll ferret it out, chapter and verse.' Kaid turned away and felt a sudden crack on his scalp before his feet gave way and the lights went out.

He came round some time later, the fierce heat of the blacksmith's fire stinging the scratches on his face.

'Lucky this guy was thereabouts or they'd be burying you back at the farm.' Seb spoke as a mug of hot coffee was thrust into Kaid's hands and the pain, by now all too familiar, shot through his head yet again.

'That boy's got no common sense.' The speaker's now familiar baritone made Kaid slowly lift his head and he found himself staring into the intense blue eyes of the mountain man. 'He can't tell when it's in his own best interest to back off.' The man threw some coins on to the table and took his horse, now fully shod, back out on to Main Street.

'That mountain man stood between you and oblivion, Kaid. Gorman's a fool but a dangerous one and you should never threaten him to his face. The mountain man's rifle stopped him in his tracks as Gorman brought his gun down a second time. Lucky for you his mount had thrown a shoe and he was heading here to have it fixed.'

'Is Gorman dead?'

'Naw. These guys know exactly where to hit and it only blasted the gun out of his hand. These guys can live without complications. He rode down and picked you up. Jude was paying his last respects to the preacher and led him back here.' Seb tidied away the tools as he spoke.

'Thought Mr Grant had told you to go out to the farm.' Kaid felt real sick.

'Was on my way when you were brought in. Do you know that guy?'

'Nodding acquaintances, Seb, that's all.'

'Saved your life. There's one you can cross off your list of suspects.'

Kaid shook his head. 'He was never on it. But I reckon I might ask him a question or two, seeing as he seems to be everywhere and sees everything that goes on.'

'Mountain men ain't big on talking. But I'm going now. I'll dampen the fire down and you keep it going quiet-like, Jude. We'll set it going real hard when we all get back. Lizzie still sulking?'

Kaid nodded and the pain shot through him yet again. 'On and off. Just mention Indiana and that'll quieten her down.'

Seb took his rifle and stopped by the door. 'You'll get nothing out of that hunter even if you were to track him down, but Jude here — well, that's a different story. Ain't nothing he doesn't hear about in Flat Stone sooner or later. Watch your back.' Kaid and Jude watched as the blacksmith rode off along the trail and Kaid settled back down by the fire, hoping the searing pain in his head would subside.

'OK, Jude, let's hear it. Beginning to

end and all points in between.'

'It ain't ended yet.'

'And I am to be alive when it does, and my pa too.'

'What do you want to know?'

'All right, kid, where do we begin? In the space of less than a day, the preacher's death was laid at my door and my pa was beaten and left for dead.'

'And you mown down.'

'Right. The common factor in all this is a McEntyre. Now you said to me you knew someone who wasn't where he should have been. Who and when — and real fast, because I feel time is running out.' Jude was a million years old and didn't have to be told twice.

'Walt Gertz, the guy who runs the saloon for Mr Rattigan.'

'When?'

'When you were bowled over by the horse. Guess he just paid some drifter to do it for him. He wasn't riding it, I'm sure of that, but nothing takes him out of Rattigan's — nothing! Yet he'd ridden out earlier that morning along the Decault Road to who knows where? Maybe to meet somebody, get his orders. Never saw when he came back.' *And then I'm hit by a horse while Gertz knifes the preacher for God only knows what reason*, thought Kaid.

'Orders from Rattigan?'

'Naw, nothing like that. Mr Rattigan's ranch is the Big Rough. He'd just send his boys in and clear things up the way he wanted them, frontier-style. Blast away everything and everybody in sight. No patience, no finesse. That's his style. He's hardly ever in these parts — prefers the territory capital. Seems Gertz is running a little business on the side. Rattigan will probably beat you to it — killing Gertz that is — if he finds out Walt's been working for somebody else on his time.'

'But why? Why my pa in all of this, for God's sake?'

'Don't know, but maybe Gertz's other boss was the one your pa was looking for. Maybe your pa knew how to flush him out.'

'And paid the price.'

'In the dark. The mark of a coward.'

'A powerful coward. But what was Pa so mad about? What's it to him what happens in Flat Stone?'

But Jude just shook his head. 'Hope you ain't figuring on going into Rattigan's and challenging Walt.'

'I ain't totally devoid of brains, kid. I just can't think how the preacher fits into all of this.' That brought back to mind the anguish in the girl's eyes as she attacked him and Kaid fingered the scratches, the dried blood streaked down his jaw.

'What did you two talk about?'

'Nothing,' answered Kaid, for it really had amounted to nothing.

'Not even about your folks and Tennessee?'

'Tennessee? But the preacher was from along the Powder River.'

'Came here from there but was born and raised in Tennessee. Maybe even knew your folks from back there. Maybe there are a lot of old scores being settled among the Tennessee boys.'

'Nope. Can't be that. My folks never said anything about the preacher and Tennessee.'

'Your pa is a man of few words. Probably didn't think it was worth mentioning. Maybe you should speak to the preacher's widow about it.'

'How come you know he was from Tennessee?'

'You should have listened out at the graveyard instead of badmouthing the sheriff.' There was obviously something in that. But Kaid shook his head, 'Can't speak to the widow right now. Wouldn't be right.' Besides Kaid wanted to stay well clear of the family till that girl calmed down. The way he saw it, he'd virtually no options. To question the preacher now he'd need a medium, and Gorman was just somebody's lackey.

'Gorman says he wasn't here when Pa was waving that knife about. That so?'

'Naw. Was watching from outside the meeting house right alongside the rev — the late reverend. I reckon he thought the mountain man would just blast away at your pa and that would be that.'

'But it didn't happen. Did you see it all?'

'Every bit of it. The mountain man rode off, the preacher moved away and the sheriff — another old Tennessee boy — hot-footed it back to Annie's cook shop. Nothing out of the ordinary.'

'Well, dead men can't speak so we'll cross the preacher off the list of helpful citizens.' Maybe he should brass it out and see the preacher's wife after all. See if McWilliams had said anything about it all to her. He'd wait and see. But his mind was made up for him right then as Jude shot up out of his chair as the late reverend's ashen-faced widow appeared grasping firmly the supporting arm of one of her sons.

'Take this chair, ma'am.'

161

Kaid turned round as the boy poked fresh life into the fire and met the piercing look of the preacher's widow. She nodded to Jude and sat down opposite Kaid. He'd half-risen as she entered and then his legs gave way and he resumed his seat. Her eyes drifted over the scratches and her face softened. 'Sorry about that.'

'I had nothing to do with your husband's death, ma'am, absolutely nothing.' The black dress highlighted her pallor and she drew a deep breath before speaking.

'I know that. The girl was wrong to do what she did and I apologize for it. I'm told your pa's ill.'

'He's not dead yet despite what this town seems to want.'

'I'm glad of that. I told my husband he should step in and do something about the way your pa was treated over at the saloon. Even if it was only because they'd all come from Tennessee . . . ' Her voice tailed off.

'Did you see Pa that night, Mrs

162

McWilliams?' The widow shook her head.

'Would you and your son here like some coffee, ma'am?' Jude hovered solicitously, aware that word of this visit would get back to Mrs Grant.

The widow smiled and refused. 'They tell me you're asking questions to find out who beat up your pa.' Kaid waited for her to go on. 'All I know is I'm not surprised it happened, that your pa broke down, that is. It had to happen sometime. All those beatings when he worked there just when Walt Gertz felt like it. My husband should have stepped in. It was his duty to try to help.' Kaid's head was splitting with pain and anger. Jerem McEntyre led two lives right enough and both were insufferable. Why did he do it? The answer to that was the answer to everything. It was Kaid's turn to breathe deeply to steady his voice.

'Mrs McWilliams, did your husband tell you anything about what my pa was doing that night?'

'Didn't mention your pa's name at all. Sorry. I'd best be going. The youngsters are taking it very badly. I came to ask that if you find out anything, Kaid, you'll let me know, won't you?'

'Should be the sheriff you're asking, ma'am.'

'We both know the value of that.'

Kaid nodded as she stood to leave. 'You'll know who killed the reverend as soon as I do, Mrs McWilliams, I promise you that. But I've a feeling he won't be in any fit state to stand trial.'

'You take care. Promise me?'

'I don't intend giving Gorman the satisfaction of watching while my pa says words over me.' His eyes followed the black-clad figure as she slowly walked back up Main Street, her arm linked through her son's for steadiness and then he mulled over her words.

'Told you he was from Tennessee.' Jude gathered up the empty mugs.

'That's right, you did. Better dampen that fire down again, Jude, or you'll have made your last pot of stew round here once Lizzie finds out you've burned down her pa's business.'

'Thinks she's the only good cook in the West. Reckon I'll join a ranch outfit. Maybe Mr Rattigan's Big Rough ranch outfit. Be more appreciated that way on the chuck wagon.' Jude looked like he was having a hard time convincing himself but his mind was made up for him as Lizzie Grant suddenly appeared.

'You can light out any time you've a mind, Jude, and the sooner the better.' Lizzie Grant missed nothing. Kaid wondered what had brought her to town — and feared the answer.

'Your pa does the hiring, Lizzie, not you!' Jude's retort was half-hearted at best.

'You've been listening to McEntyre here too much, all mouth and nothing else. Now see to the horse.' She looked into the cold coffee pot and shook the dregs about. 'Anybody thought to put on something to eat?' she asked pointedly. 'The world's greatest cook, maybe?' Her long look of contempt would have shattered a lesser person than Jude but he stood his ground, although it was Kaid who answered. 'Nope.' Kaid wondered what had brought her back but steered clear of asking her. Jude had no such inhibitions.

'You're back because you're sweet on Kaid.' The coffee dregs smacked off the boy's face, the dark, thick liquid soaking his curly brown hair.

'Stick to stoking fires! Now shove off and dry off. I want to speak to him.' Jude was nobody's fool and regretted forgetting that Lizzie Grant had no sense of humour. Lizzie waited until she could see him over by the stables. 'Your pa's been talking — in a garbled sort of way. My pa thought you should know.'

'How is Pa?' It had only been a few hours but death was a frequent and sudden visitor in that territory.

'Better.'

Kaid relaxed visibly. 'A mountain

man anywhere near the farm?'

'No. Pa's trigger-finger's a bit nervous so it's better nobody comes close and Seb will be there by now. Passed him on the trail to your place. Is this guy trouble?'

'Not till Pa's back on his feet. What's Pa been saying, Lizzie? Must have been something smart to get your attention.' The coffee pot was still in her hand and Kaid was prepared to duck. She laid it down carefully by the fire.

'Nothing we could make out. We were hoping he'd maybe say who'd beaten him up. Asked him but it didn't seem to matter. Just names, family names maybe, over and over again.'

'The children's?'

'No, nor your ma's neither. Nathan Chesney, over and over again. Does that mean anything to you?'

'Nothing.'

'Asked him if that was who'd done it, but he just fell back on to the pillow and shut his eyes. Nothing more.'

'Nathan Chesney.' It rang no bells in

the deepest reaches of Kaid's mind as he said the name slowly over and over again.

'So what do you figure on doing?'

'No real idea. Guess I might as well start all over again. Probably at Rattigan's. The one guy in this town who knows what it's all about is Walt Gertz, I'm sure of that.'

'Ain't where I would start.' Kaid sighed as she spoke. Lizzie Grant was too opinionated but this could take some time and he needed feeding. He waited for her to continue and knew she needed no prompting. 'Gorman's the weak link here. Takes orders, never gives them. Sign of a weak character. Start on him. He's got a big mouth and likes the sounds of his own voice. He'll give something away even if he doesn't realize it.'

'Keep listening and thinking, Lizzie. I reckon you're wasted at that stove after all.'

7

Lizzie Grant was right, Kaid reckoned. Gorman would slip up at some point because he couldn't let anybody have the last word. Let him dig a hole and bury himself in it. Why had he lied over his whereabouts? Standing with the preacher. What could be more innocent? Kaid's eyes sought out the jailhouse and saw the hitching rail empty. He kept right on walking, for a good guess said that a man of Gorman's physique lent itself to more than his fair share of grub and the only eating-house in town where he'd fit in and probably get fed free was Annie's cook shop run by the owner of the bawdy houses. It was a good move by Annie — no botheration where the employees were concerned. Annie's girls were discreetly out of sight and Annie herself supervized the slapping down of piled tin plates before hungry cowboys and general riff-raff. The batwings spoke of the shop's former existence as a saloon before competition and public decency laws effected a change of usage. The food was no better than the cheap liquor it had once sold but it had its dedicated clientele, of whom Gorman was head boy. The jailhouse was obviously not the place to find the sheriff as of that moment, and Kaid knew it was a fair bet, as his deputy's horse was hitched outside Annie's, that Gorman was somewhere in the vicinity, his horse probably round the back. Old habits again. They were likely to get a man killed. Kaid breasted the batwings and was ignored by one and all — except the deputy. 'Your pa dead yet?'

'Lizzie Grant's back to make supper for her folks, like you hadn't noticed. What does that tell you?'

'Tells me you'd best get back to that dirt farm and bury your pa. Sure don't want dead folks lying about in this heat.'

'Where's the sheriff?'

'That what you come to tell him?'

'Ain't come to tell him anything.'

'Well, he's got all the help he needs, two deputies and all the folks round here more than willing to pitch in when needed. And we've especially got no jobs round here for dirt farmers who ain't got no dirt to farm. Seems I heard tell your mortgage ain't been paid and that means you McEntyres are squatters.'

A frown creased Kaid's face. 'Where is he?'

'Out back.' Out back covered a multitude of sins in that particular area of Flat Stone and Kaid hoped it was a minor call of nature and not a prolonged courtesy call on one of Annie's young ladies.

'I'll wait.'

'You wait, you eat.' Annie's hard face hove into view. 'This ain't the jailhouse. I've got a living to make.'

'Got no money for luxuries, ma'am.' Kaid's soft smile cut no ice with Annie and a slight nod of her head turned things real nasty in the cook shop. 'Could be embarrassing if I went out back right now to speak to him, ma'am.' Annie's little helpers edged in on him and Kaid wondered if this was the time to see how fast he could draw from a holster. 'A law-abiding citizen just wanting a word with the town lawman — folks round here are edgy enough with their preacher murdered to not be prepared to put up with a crime outbreak. Liable to close down this entire side of Main Street — meeting house excepted, naturally. Am I worth the loss?' Another almost imperceptible nod of the head and things returned to normal in the cook shop.

'What word do you want with the law? As the sheriff's temporarily out of it, I'm the one to speak to,' advised the deputy.

'Somebody kicked hell out of my pa

and I want to know what's being done about it.'

'Your pa's dead. End of the trail,' the deputy butted in.

'Makes no difference to me. I still want to know who beat him up and why.'

'He was making a damned nuisance of himself all the time. Asking for it.'

'My pa was a decent man and it seems to me he's due some justice here.'

'And he'll get it. Right, boys, mount up and we'll all go help bury his pa.'

Kaid's fist cracked off the deputy's jaw, his boot hoisting him right out of the chair he'd been lolling against. Annie's Navy Colt came from nowhere and her henchmen bundled Kaid through the batwings like a well-drilled army.

'You bleed all over my godamned floor, Deputy, and you're a dead man.' Kaid heard her low threat as he picked himself off the ground and hared off like greased lightning, Jude several

173

yards ahead of him. Within minutes, he was mounted and heading along the Decault Road as fast as Ellie Grant's horse would take him, for Kaid now knew he'd been wasting his time — or letting the deputy deliberately waste it for him. Gorman wasn't in Flat Stone. Like the deputy said, he was out at the farm making sure Pa had breathed his last and it could be Pa was now dead, right enough.

Lizzie Grant would know by now, for the ever-present Jude, who'd been lurking outside Annie's, would have made a beeline for her as Kaid had made straight for the horse. Kaid expected her to storm past him any minute, for her horsemanship was superb and he was no match for her in that area. He hoped like hell her folks had done nothing foolish. The horse was a good one when asked and they were within a mile of the dirt farm turn-off when Lizzie sped past. Not a word was exchanged between them.

Cutting away from the Decault Road,

he rounded the last bend before the farm, small bluffs lining the trail at this point, and suddenly he had to rein in sharply. Lizzie was nowhere in sight but Gorman's men were. Silent and morose, their way was blocked by the mountain men, four of them strung across the trail, huge and forbidding astride their mounts, rifles loaded and no doubt primed to fire the minute Gorman's men tried to pass. But there was no sign of the young guy — nor of Gorman nor Eyton, his other ever-present deputy.

'Things to be settled back there, son. Best you stay here — and live.'

'I'm going past.'

The mountain man, the one who'd done all the speaking in Rattigan's, slowly shook his head.

'No you ain't. Won't do you any good. You'll be let past when certain matters are brought to a conclusion.' His eyes were riveting and Kaid thought there was indeed no way of getting past them at that point. He made to wheel his horse about. It was a wide-open valley, so there were other places, plenty of them.

'Don't even consider it, son.' The rifle was brought to bear on Ellie's horse and Kaid eased his mount back facing the mountain men.

'Where's the girl?'

'Didn't come past here or we would have stopped her. Her kin at the cabin?' Kaid nodded. 'Smart kid.'

'Is Gorman back there?'

'He is.'

'And you let him through?'

'The sheriff and his deputy were on lawful business. No reason not to.'

'And these men?'

'Don't like crowds. Tends to blur the issue. They're free to ride on if they want to. Already told them so — if they want to commit suicide, obviously, and it seems none of them does.' Whatever was happening back there at the farm, the mountain men were deeply involved and Kaid's fear for his pa rose relentlessly in him.

'My pa's in no fit state to defend himself,' he argued.

'Right now, son, your pa don't figure in this.' His last words exploded in Kaid's ears along with a sudden outburst of gunfire which rang out from the direction of the farm. 'Don't move — don't even breathe hard.' More followed, rifle mixed with handgun. A lifetime of silence hung in the hot air and no movement among the men on the road could be detected, Gorman's men uneasy, the mountain men listening intently. Two more shots rang out in deliberate fashion, but this time only a rifle spoke.

'Reckon you guys had better ride back to town and tell the other deputy he'd better bring out a buckboard.' He didn't have to say it twice and Kaid was left on his own. 'You'd better move, too, son. It's your family's farm.'

Kaid had their company on the short distance to the cabin, his mind half-reassured somehow by these hard men at his side and half-terrified by the thought of what the shots had meant. They'd said his pa wasn't involved and that made no sense, as it was clear to him now that the two rifle shots had been the signal they were waiting for and that they'd probably been fired by the youngest of their group. His vow was to kill Pa but Pa was still too ill for it to be an honourable contest. So who else out there had been on his list? Only the lawmen, the Grants and Seb should have been there. He hoped to God Lizzie had used the brain she was so proud of and stayed well clear of it all. But her horse was out back of the cabin and that put paid to that hope.

They slowed automatically and Kaid's eyes went to the form of the young mountain man sitting easily in the saddle, his rifle butt resting on his right thigh, his finger still on the trigger. His eyes never left the prone form of the sheriff until his comrades were once more at his side. Mr Grant stood over the lawman, his wife at the cabin door, white sheet already in her hands. Seb was leading the two lawmen's mounts to the hitching rail, Gorman's deputy was seated, head in hands, on the steps leading to the cabin.

'The deputy shot Gorman dead,' stated John Grant, as though he was just quoting the price of a new wheel-rim.

'It was an accident. Was aiming for him.' The deputy glanced sourly at the mountain man and that brought a smile to the faces of those tough men. 'The sheriff just got in the way.'

'There was no need to aim at anybody.' John Grant was in no mood to console him. 'They rode in here just after Seb, all fired up to take Jerem McEntyre back to Flat Stone — one way or another.'

'Where's Pa?' Kaid asked anxiously as he dismounted.

'Back there. Lizzie's with him.' Mrs Grant spoke as she carefully covered the inert body of the sheriff. 'Your pa's all right.' Kaid's eyes went to the mountain man but he'd already wheeled his horse about and was riding off with the others.

'What happened?'

'Don't rightly know and I sure as hell don't understand.' John Grant watched as his wife did her best to cover Gorman up. Kaid realized that his chance of finding out what Gorman knew had now vanished.

'Guess we should get him back to town.'

'There'll be no dead men in our buggy! You'd best use one of the horses and that old buckboard back there.' Ellie Grant had definite ideas on the use of Grant transport.

'No need, Mrs Grant. The mountain men had stopped the rest of the posse on the trail till it was all over and then sent them back to tell the other deputy to bring a buckboard out here for Gorman. Well, they didn't actually name the sheriff.'

'How did they know?'

Kaid shook his head. 'Guess the two rifle shots said it was all over. Anyway, best leave him right there. And him, too. Have you got his gun?'

The deputy's face was a mixture of rage and misery, each feeling battling the other for supremacy. 'Right here.'

'It was an accident,' protested Eyton again to no one in particular. 'Gorman's horse reared and the sheriff got in my firing line.'

'Lucky for you he did, for that mountain man had you dead to rights.' John Grant scowled as he spoke.

'Yeah, and we heard you the last time, Deputy,' said Kaid sourly. 'Why was that hunter here, Mr Grant? Did he say?'

'Not a word, Kaid. He and his horse just ambled on down, rifle sheathed, hands spread to show he had no gun in his hand. Didn't figure he'd cause trouble since Seb told me he'd helped you out with Gorman at the church-yard.'

'Did he try to see Pa?'

'Didn't come any closer than you saw. Just sat there and waited.'

'Was he waiting for Gorman?'

The blacksmith shrugged his shoulders. 'Can't figure out why. Must've been something private if he was. Guess they must have been watching his every move and saw their chance when he left town.'

'The rest of the mountain men were about half a mile back, keeping the posse there,' said Kaid.

'Yeah, Gorman said that. So what was it all about?' The silence that followed answered that question.

'Did Gorman try to see Pa?'

'Yeah, but my wife was having none of it. Too sick, she said, but Gorman paid her no heed. Came riding right on in.'

'We heard a lot of shots fired.'

'The mountain man spoke to Gorman. Wanted a word with him.'

'About what?'

'No idea. But Gorman started to badmouth him. He'd already drawn his gun and was waving it around like the ass he was. He was a foul-mouthed guy right enough. I told him myself to hush up. Women present. The mountain man just sat there. No threat to anybody, it seemed, so I guess that encouraged Gorman to show off. But I got the distinct feeling a bullet from the hunter's rifle had Gorman's name on it all the time — in a manner of speaking. As soon as the sheriff began to dismount, I'm sure I heard a rifle shot. Must have slipped it out as Gorman was cracking bad jokes about him with the deputy. Guess a bullet from that was what spooked the horse. Probably aimed it at the ground in front of Gorman's horse. Eyton there had been very nervous all along and the least thing was bound to set him off. My guess is that guy sensed it and got him to do his work for him.'

'He's still got more important business to finish — with my pa, I mean. Do you reckon Gorman just got in his way?'

'No chance. He knew who he was

waiting for. He got him and he rode off.'

'Sure he said nothing?'

'Ask Lizzie. She spoke to him as she walked her horse past him. Probably told her to keep on going.'

'She knew those mountain men would be here. That's what I don't understand. The logical way here was the Decault Road and the turn-off but she never went near there. How could she have possibly known? She didn't leave Flat Stone till Jude told her the sheriff was heading out here.'

'Only one way to find out. Ask her. She's back there with your pa.'

Kaid took a last glance back at the shroud-covered form and cursed the fact that the mountain man had manipulated Gorman's death. He'd now lost his chance to question him.

'I'll see to the horse.' Seb led the animal away and Kaid tried to frame the questions he'd put to Lizzie that would get the answers in the shortest possible time. He'd business in Flat

Stone and what few options he had were vanishing fast. But first he had to talk to Pa.

Lizzie was helping his pa to take some soup and Kaid was relieved to see the extreme pallor topped now by eyes that had lost their faraway look.

'A word, Lizzie.' Pa's eyes closed as she gently let his frail body rest once more against the pillows. They moved over to the window — the grime of the past few years now removed, no doubt by Mrs Grant. Kaid looked at the majestic grandeur of the distant mountains as they rose out of the fertile valley. Only the extreme edge of the valley failed to benefit from the Crazy River's abundant flow, only this part was parched and impotent, as the life-giving rains always saved their bounty until their clouds met the highest parts of the Sephina Range many miles away.

'Can't figure it out, Lizzie.'

'Figure what out?' She knew what but she was giving him no help.

'How you knew the mountain men would be right round that bend. There was nothing to indicate it.'

The silence that followed could have been cut with a knife.

'Never was one for the obvious. Trails are for the unimaginative.'

'OK, so let me use my imagination, let it roam wild and free. That help, Lizzie?'

'Be more interesting, yes. Sure you're up to it?'

'I guess I am. Like to think so anyway. You suggested I talk to Gorman. Now if I was a real suspicious character, I'd say you'd sent me on a wild-goose chase. Me going one way, while Gorman goes the other.' Lizzie leaned against the window-frame and listened, her eyes never leaving Kaid's face.

'Can see how you might reach that conclusion.'

'But the only trouble is, you didn't know Gorman was headed in this direction and had already left. Jude messed up badly there.'

'He was too busy watching you. Coming along Main Street, I'd heard Gorman was going out to the Triple X and thought hanging about Annie's might just keep you out of trouble for a bit. You got no experience, Kaid. Likely to get yourself killed. But I never reckoned he'd go to the farm with Pa there. Forgot he was a real dumb guy.' Lizzie shrugged as she went on. 'I guessed the other deputies would be strung out along the trail to give Gorman and Eyton a free hand if you did happen along. An educated guess was all it was.'

'And out there, Lizzie. What did the mountain man say to you at the cabin? Your pa said you spoke to him.'

'It was all very edgy. The sheriff was sounding off, telling the mountain man to move or he'd gun him down for interfering with the law. Pa's trigger-finger was jumpy and Ma came running out to head me off round the back. She was sure Gorman would be happy to shoot anybody with a gun of any kind and didn't want me caught in the crossfire. Gorman was itching for an excuse and Pa was sweating blood trying to calm him down. Gorman was demanding your pa be put in the buckboard and driven back to the jailhouse. My pa wouldn't budge and the hunter just sat there, watching, but he'd silently unsheathed the rifle as the others argued and held it over his arm. He did it in a split second; smooth as silk his action was, and I think I was the only one who saw it.'

'So what did he say to you? Were you in his way?'

'Do I look stupid? I ain't never walked in front of a rifle in my life. He motioned me round behind him and as I passed — very slowly — he didn't even turn his head. But I heard his words just the same. The others didn't but I did. All he said was, 'Tell him Nathan was here and I'll be back to finish it off'.' Nathan Chesney! Lizzie smiled as Kaid then spoke quietly.

'The name Pa said.'

'Well, your pa knows he's been here, too, for I told him. Whether the news was good or bad, I don't know. And before you go mad, it was his right to know. His eyes were closed but he rubbed them free of tears just the same.'

Kaid brutally crushed that image and kept his temper well under control.

'You can take it from me it's bad. Seems like he's working through a list and both Pa and the sheriff were or are on it. I ain't got any chance now of getting Gorman to talk. Looks like Pa's got two men on his trail. How the hell did he manage that?'

'So what you're now trying to do is look for Walt Gertz to spill the beans on who is employing both Gertz and the sheriff — was, in the sheriff's case.'

'Do you think Rattigan knows about their sidelines, Lizzie?'

'There would be two dead guys and not one if he did. He's more taken up with territory politics than a backwater like Flat Stone Creek. Gertz is just making hay while the sun shines. As long as the saloon's profits are still on the rise, their boss will have no reason to complain or be suspicious. Walt Gertz is one smart guy but he'll be watching his back just the same.' Lizzie had a grudging admiration for smartness but somehow no sign of it crept into her voice when she mentioned Gertz's name.

Kaid moved over to kneel beside his pa. 'Pa, I know you're hurting but I also know you can hear me. When this is all over, you'd better tell me all about it from start to finish or, God help me, I'll kill you myself.' His pa's eyes were covered by his hands and the bruising along his arms and face were stomach-churning.

'Let him rest.' Lizzie's scowl warned Kaid to back off, but he hadn't finished.

'Nathan Chesney says he's come here to finish it but I'll keep faith with you and try to stop him.' His pa's hand suddenly grabbed Kaid's wrist and he shook his head violently. But a fit of coughing brought Mrs Grant hurrying in.

'Out! Both of you! Lizzie, you should know better.'

'I was just talking to my pa, Mrs Grant,' pleaded Kaid but the unpredictable Lizzie butted in.

'And threatening to kill him. Ma, he's mad. The sooner you leave Flat Stone the better, Kaid McEntyre. We'll take your pa in at our place till he's well, won't we Ma?'

'I guess we'll do that right now. John! Seb!' Ellie Grant called through to the men folk. 'Fix up that buckboard right away. Seb, you wait here with the deputy and Gorman's body till the rest of them get here. And don't let them touch a thing in this cabin. It's McEntyre property.'

Kaid knew he'd no time to spare. He wanted to see what reaction there had been in Flat Stone to his information that his pa was dead.

'The buckboard will take an hour or two to fix, Ellie. Ain't safe to use in the condition it's in and that buggy would be agony for Jerem all cooped up.'

Mrs Grant gave way to her husband's superior knowledge. 'Then I'll make us all supper while you two do it. By that time they'll be back from Flat Stone to take the lawman and his killer back.' She glared at the deputy and he flinched visibly. 'And if I know that other lazy good-for-nothing of a deputy, he'll take his time.'

But Kaid had no time for eating. He wanted a word with the only guy in town left alive who knew what this was all about. Walt Gertz was the next on Kaid McEntyre's list, but first Kaid had a bit of bad news to deliver to the deputy.

8

Kaid rode easy into Flat Stone and was conscious of the clouds now gathering overhead. The weather looked as if it might break shortly and the farm would be awash in red mud. His plans for a future well away from the valley were lost somewhere in the events of the past few hours. Kaid's trouble was isolation — the result of which had left him with very little understanding of the Flat Stone social scene. Everybody in these parts was better placed to know the late sheriff, his acquaintances and his history than Kaid.

'Heard your pa's dead.' Kaid tipped the world-weary Stetson he'd picked up on the trail years before as the wagon trundled past him. The woman had already turned away to speak to her husband and Kaid reckoned that was about what the McEntyres were worth in these parts. Four short words delivered with neither sympathy nor concern. The answer that was about to spring to his lips died immediately. Alive or dead, nobody cared, except the person who'd thought he'd accomplished the dead part the previous day.

Kaid's eyes narrowed as the trail in front sloped down to meet the first of Flat Stone's shacks and houses some half a mile ahead. He should have passed the buckboard heading back towards the farm with the other deputy right alongside it. They should've set out long since to fetch back the sheriff or Eyton, dead or wounded, it didn't matter. That other deputy was obviously in no way greatly concerned. Dead or wounded men didn't go anywhere and he'd pick both lawmen up at leisure.

Kaid decided that he'd better reinforce the fact that he didn't want corpses sprouting up all over land he'd just tilled. The deputy was about to get a visit from him and somehow Kaid felt very vulnerable as he checked the Peacemaker once more. It made him nervous, just the very weight of it all about his waist and he glanced again at the beauty of the JK holster. There was no way he was going to back anybody into a corner. There was no way he was going to end up dead because of loose talk. Kaid McEntyre had nothing against anybody right then and his tongue would be kept firmly under control at all times. He was poor, ill-educated and resentful but he was very definitely not stupid. If the town thought his pa was dead, maybe the guy Pa had tried to flush out would now oblige and show himself, just to make sure and Kaid meant to stay alive long enough to meet him.

But first he had to figure out a way to find out more about the late, unlamented sheriff. Kaid had no way of knowing whether once it was thought Pa was dead, Kaid himself wouldn't be next on the list. He was young and fit and had no suicidal intentions. It was time to think fast.

'What happened?' Jude appeared from nowhere as Kaid dismounted outside the blacksmith's. Kaid accepted the cup of strong, black coffee and knelt down opposite the fire. Jude nudged it back into life and Kaid watched the embers awake and take on a welcoming orange glow.

'Nothing.'

'It's me — Jude.' The boy's annoyance showed clearly on his face at being locked out of Kaid's thoughts.

'Nothing,' Kaid repeated.

'Your pa dead right enough then?' Jude asked quietly.

'Nope, but you don't know that.' Kaid's keen blue eyes seared into Jude as he spoke and the kid nodded. He had a right to know and Kaid knew he could trust him.

'Is Gorman still out there?'

'For the time being. The mountain men stopped the posse from going on to Pa's land, that's all. They decided Gorman and Eyton could make a reasonable case on their own.'

'Posse said they heard shots but when the mountain men rode in here casual-like a while later, they just reckoned what they'd heard meant nothing.'

'Would've thought the deputy might have checked it out,' said Kaid.

'Naw, the mountain men rode into Flat Stone and the deputy reckoned that if anything had happened to Gorman, they'd have steered well clear of town. He guessed the sheriff was being fed by Mrs Grant.'

'Lazy swine was just looking for an excuse to grab an extra sleep in the jailhouse, I reckon.'

Jude nodded. 'Sounds like him.'

'Is that where he is right now?' asked McEntyre, drinking deeply from the large cup.

'Yeah. Said Gorman and Eyton expected to escort Mr Grant and the others back here.'

'Pa too?'

'Never mentioned your pa, Kaid.'

'Probably expected I'd do like he told me and bury him.'

'A sheriff ain't paid to do that,' Jude declared authoritatively, having once contemplated that career path himself, it seemed.

'I guess not.'

'You'd best do what you have to do before Gorman rides into Flat Stone and arrests you for murdering your pa — courtesy of a bullet from him, for if you left your pa alive and Gorman still out there, that's what might have happened. An accident, of course.' Kaid laughed and Jude frowned.

'I'll take your advice but I'm in no hurry.'

'He's dead, ain't he? Gorman?' Lizzie Grant's intuition had rubbed off on Jude.

'You're gonna stay right here, Jude, and tend the fire like you were told. Anybody comes a-calling, you vanish. Lizzie's an unforgiving sort and if she learns you got in my way . . . ' Kaid didn't have to finish.

'Did you shoot him?' The very idea that Jude thought him able to outgun anybody cheered him up.

'Was nowhere near the farm when it happened. I was talking to the posse and the mountain men at the time. It was an accident, that's all. Deputy did it. But remember, you talk to nobody about any of this. This place isn't open for business. That's what the notice says and you'd better make sure your mouth stays closed as well.'

Jude looked hurt at the inference and Kaid immediately regretted his threatening tone. Once he stepped outside, he himself would be the one guy folk reckoned they could put down at will. 'I need to know there's somebody who'll help me if it all goes wrong. I'm relying on you to stand firm, Jude.'

Jude understood. 'Lizzie would have got her pa to throttle me if she didn't think she or any of her kin could count on me when the chips were down.'

'I know that. I'll be back. In the

meantime, is there anything I should know?' Kaid had walked over to the half-open doors and stopped, taking in the scene before him.

'You'd better get in as much of what you want to do quickly before the deputy gets up off his lazy butt and heads for your place. He'll have to do it sooner or later.'

'I intend to.' But where should he begin, Kaid wondered.

'Goin' to Annie's cook shop might help you.'

That advice surprised Kaid. 'In what way?'

'Annie and Gorman were real close. Real close.' Kaid smiled at Jude.

'Jude, if you could cook like Lizzie, John Grant would never know that sharp-brained gal had gone to Indiana. Thank God for curiosity. Be seein' you.'

'Don't draw that gun unless you feel real lucky, Kaid.'

Kaid's new-found confidence dipped slightly as reality sank in and he began walking up Main Street towards

Annie's cook shop. His original intention of announcing Gorman's demise was now firmly on the back-burner. Gorman's activities outwith the sheriff's office were his target and if, as Jude had stated, he and Annie had had something going between them, it was reasonable to assume she might know what he did in his spare time and who he did it for. He felt uneasy for he knew that he'd be bringing her bad news and he also knew he'd release that information when it suited his own ends with no regard whatsoever for the woman's feelings.

He stopped at the hitching post outside the building and was aware of the preacher's family progressing his way. He waited and touched the brim of his hat as they passed silently by. With hope rising within him, he entered the still-busy eating-house. Annie pounced.

'You again? Stew or Irish stew?'

Kaid looked about him as he answered: 'What's the difference?'

'The price.'

'I ain't hungry, no ma'am.'

'Batwings are still slapping hell out of each other. Keep them going.' Annie dismissed Kaid from her sight and mind.

'Like a word, ma'am.'

She turned back to him. 'There's only one — stew. Otherwise, I'm deaf. On your way, son.' Annie's head moved very slightly but if it had been the Liberty Bell, it couldn't have made a bigger impression on the huge guys standing each side of the batwings.

'Take it easy. It's a word you'll want to hear, ma'am. It's about the sheriff and who he's been associating with lately.' Stew, Irish or otherwise, lost its appeal immediately and Kaid followed the lady into her private office, the door being deliberately left open. Her expression was even fiercer now and Kaid wondered how this female hardcase could have latched on to a vapid loser like Gorman. Even the mothering instinct of the species couldn't account for it. He had the horrible feeling he'd voluntarily entered the lioness's den.

'What do you know about my brother?' This piece of information succeeded in corkscrewing Kaid's brain, but as he had been in the process of walking towards the chair she'd indicated, Annie didn't see his expression change. Gorman the loser was out, impartial enforcer of the law was in. The bad news might never cross his lips while he was in that room, or the cook shop come to that, as the two burly 'friends' materialized right then in his mind's eye. Decision one — almost made. But years of speaking only the words that needed saying held firm and they were out before he could readjust his way of thinking.

'He's dead, ma'am. It happened out at our farm.' Kaid's hands now held no aces. He'd blown it and in the shocked silence that followed, he realized he'd now run out of options.

'You do it?' She was gazing down, unseeingly he supposed, at some papers on her desk. Her voice had lost its cutting edge.

'Nope. It was an accident. I wasn't even there.' Her head came up and her eyes narrowed, and he hurried on before the unseen 'friends' were somehow summoned into the inner sanctum. 'Deputy was nervous.'

'Fred Eyton always was.'

'Your brother's horse reared.'

'Bloody idiot was no horseman.'

Kaid soldiered on as his grip on the situation unravelled with every interruption from the less than devastated sister. 'It reared and somehow Eyton thought it spelled trouble and fired. The Grants were all there. They saw what happened — out on our farm,' he repeated. 'Guess he'd gone there to speak to my pa.'

'Shot by his own deputy.' There was silence for a minute or two before Annie spoke again. 'Have you brought him back to Flat Stone?'

'No ma'am. The posse had been told to bring out a buckboard. They haven't done it yet. I guess they didn't realize the true significance of the shots. Probably thought that the deputy, the nervous one, had just got nicked. They were still on the trail. Never quite reached the farm.'

'I'll soon make them see it,' she said and Kaid didn't doubt that for a minute. 'Thanks for letting me know.'

'Must admit I had a second reason for coming. But under the circumstances . . . ' His voice faltered. 'I didn't realize you were blood kin.'

But Annie was no sentimentalist. 'He owned half of this and now I own it all.' She smiled brightly as she spoke. 'Nice little town that's sure to get bigger as the railroad comes along. Bound to, sooner or later. With what's coming to me I can expand. Maybe buy some land further up the valley. But you want to know what he was up to and who was paying him. Or was I not supposed to know about the trips? Were you about to tell me he was meeting somebody on the sly — me being his girlfriend, you supposed? Jealous lady-friend would then spill the beans, was that it? That what you hoped for?'

'I suppose it was. My mistake,' said Kaid, embarrassed. But suddenly Annie seemed to lose the joy that the initial feeling of financial freedom had brought her as the reality of the situation sank in. An odd look of vulnerability crept into her manner. 'But Ned was the only kin I got — there's nobody now, dumb or otherwise. Kin is kin so I'll get that other deputy to do his duty.' She spoke softly and straightened the papers in front of her with very little interest in them.

'Let me tell him, ma'am.'

'All right, but you come right back. Maybe my memory will be better.'

Kaid nodded and hoped like hell it was her judgement that would improve. It was him against her loyalty to a loud-mouthed nonentity of a brother but, as Annie had said and Kaid knew to his cost, kin was kin.

Once more he was back in the street,

this time the shadows were lengthening, the thunderclouds overhead more in keeping with the season. Kaid had a farmer's eye and he knew it. Knew it and hated himself for it. He'd get a job in a store, he decided. Big white apron, wrap candy for the kids and smile at every man, woman and child who came through the door with money in their pockets. It could heave it down with rain all day long and it wouldn't bother him one bit. The inside of that store would be his life.

A peal of thunder echoed along the valley and habit made him look away to the horizon, away to the endless dust and the cabin where his pa lay hurting. His eyes glanced back along the row of stores on either side of the jailhouse and his stomach heaved at the new thought of being incarcerated indoors for the rest of his days. Somehow he wondered where the mountain men were right then. Rattigan's probably. Wouldn't leave, he'd bet, till the young one had had his revenge or died trying.

Kaid took a deep breath and breezed into the jailhouse with its rows of spare badges and Wanted posters lining the walls.

'Well, if it ain't the farmer boy!' Another weasel face leered at Kaid.

'And wearing a gun!' said one even uglier, squaring up to Kaid. McEntyre had the feeling the gun was definitely bad news — for him.

'Best you bury your pa yourself, son, for as you know better than anybody, the Reverend Ben McWillians is unavailable.' The deputy sniggered at his own joke.

'I ain't here to discuss McEntyre business and you should show a bit more respect for your fellow citizens. I reckon the preacher's widow has more clout round here than you, mister.'

The deputy's face hardened. 'You here to turn yourself in? Lock him up, Joe. There's a few lice-ridden drunks in there to keep him company. If they object, too bad.'

'Turn myself in for what?'

'Where do we start, boys?'

'The preacher,' suggested one help-fully.

'And wasting the sheriff's time complaining about being run down by a horse. When he gets back, he'll string you up.' Those guys were just full of ideas.

'Maybe this guy beat up his own pa. There was always bad blood between them.'

Kaid didn't rise to the bait. A lifetime on a dirt farm taught patience and he was suddenly very grateful for that. If he went for his gun, he'd be doing exactly what they were trying to goad him into doing.

'So what is it, McEntyre?' The deputy took control yet again.

'Would just like to know who hired a nobody like you?' McEntyre was getting used to living dangerously.

'Sheriff Gorman hired me and I ain't no nobody. You either get a grip on that mouth of yours or you'll find that out real fast. Now, you've known who hired

209

me for ever, boy, so why ask such a stupid question now?'

'But why you? How come he picked you out of ten other guys who probably went for the job? A quiet town like this is no trouble. Money rolls right into your pocket for just sitting there on your ass.'

'Lots of drifters, traders. Can get a bit rough at times.'

'It ain't Tombstone.'

'Could be heading that way if you McEntyres don't hit the trail.'

'But why you? Old sidekicks, is that it?' Kaid wasn't about to put all his eggs in one basket this time. Annie might not come through. She might just talk or, more likely as she had business aspirations in Flat Stone, clam up permanently. Even if she did talk, it might not amount to a hill o' beans.

'Ned and me go back a long way,' rasped the deputy. Kaid made a leap of faith.

'The old Tennessee days, right?' he suggested.

'Right.'

'How come the old Tennessee bonds hold sway round here?' It was a puzzle Kaid realized might be at the heart of the whole business. 'Did nothing for us.'

'Stopped you being evicted from that dirt farm.' Kaid's feet felt like lead and firmly rooted to the ground. He said nothing, hoped the deputy was enjoying his position of power too much to stop. 'Who else but a warm-hearted guy from Tennessee like Mr Rattigan would give a dirt farmer a job just to stop fellow Tennessee folks from becoming homeless? If it hadn't been for that job, you'd have lost your home — such as it is — long since. That land on its own couldn't have paid the church collection, never mind a mortgage. Your pa was real lucky to get it. Cantankerous devil never showed any gratitude. I guess that means you're homeless now since your pa can't keep up the payments, and you're such a loud-mouth, nobody round here would employ you.'

Kaid McEntyre accepted at last that there had been a mortgage.

'How come you know so much about McEntyre business?'

'The sheriff told me last night over a plate of Irish stew. Was full of it. I expect the owner will want to repossess, red dust and all.'

'He'll have no trouble from me. But talking about the dead, until the owner appears, I'm still farming that land and the only dead I want on it are McEntyres. Now I'll say this once, so you'd better listen as your boys obviously paid no heed to the mountain men. Get Gorman's body the hell off my land.' The deputy rose quickly out of his chair as Kaid's bullet drilled a hole through a deputy's badge on the opposite wall.

'You won't need it any more. You can have Gorman's till they appoint another sheriff. You all got it? He's dead. Shot by his own deputy in front of witnesses. Maybe next time they'll wise up and hire some guy from Kentucky.' The

Peacemaker slipped sweetly into the JK holster and Kaid McEntyre slipped equally unhindered out of the door, leaving behind him the shattered confidence of the lawman. He'd aimed for the sheriff's badge, but who was to know that but himself?

The first spatter of rain fell as he crossed back to Annie's. He saw Seb trundle up Main Street, Ellie Grant's buggy crammed with Eyton and the shrouded figure of Ned Gorman, and turn into the undertaker's yard. Ellie had obviously relented when faced with a decaying corpse on her hands. The rain wouldn't come to much but it would cool the air a little. Kaid hoped Annie would come up with a fact or two, for he was seriously short of proof of anything. So that was why Pa had worked at Rattigan's. Maybe there was some sense beginning to appear. After Annie, Walt Gertz was next on the list.

The heavy guys made to stop him but Annie motioned him to a table at the back of the cook shop, well away from the others. Immediately a plate of stew and potatoes was placed in front of him, thick slices of bread already dipped in the gravy.

'Best stew in town.'

Kaid nodded in agreement as he ate on and appreciated Jude's talent a little more. 'Real filling, ma'am.'

'And hot like it should be. Aim to buy myself a nice little spread in the foothills of the Sephinas. I'll get somebody in to run it for me while I expand this place.'

'Takes money.'

'My brother was an idiot in general but he wasn't one with money. Got a tidy bit stashed away and I know where it is.'

'For keeping his mouth shut and running errands?' Annie nodded as she replied.

'It's mounted up to quite a bit over the years and the spread I have in mind ain't big — yet. This place is a gold mine, so I'm quite nicely placed financially.'

Kaid's heart sank at the thought of a clever woman who so obviously had achieved more than all the McEntyres put together. Again the old resentment surfaced and it was even harder to bear this time, knowing that they hadn't even owned the land outright. His appetite left him.

'On the house,' Annie said as Kaid put down his spoon on the empty plate. Thank God for that, he thought, for paying wasn't an option right then.

'Many thanks.' There was a quietness about the cook shop, trade having slackened as the late afternoon approached. It would pick up again in an hour or two but right then, Annie had other things on her mind.

'You told them about Ned?' She asked him.

'Yeah.' There'd been no activity across the road; the lawmen's horses were hitched there as usual. That suited Kaid, for the longer the news that his pa was still alive was kept from the general public, the better. He had a few hours to get to the bottom of it all but no more. 'Just saw Seb Reilly take your brother's body into the Clements brothers' place as I came over. Guess one of your guys should go over and inform the lawmen there's no need to go out to the farm any more.'

Annie nodded and left, returning a few minutes later, a black shawl suitably draped over her slim shoulders.

'Have you thought any more about what we were discussing?' he asked. He took a long draught of the coffee and it was remarkably good. Kaid couldn't remember ever having eaten in a cook shop of any description before and the thought of enjoying doing so now, when Pa was still so weak, caused a rush of guilt coursing through him.

'Ned was always getting the nod from Gertz to go on little errands. Always riding out at night. At first I'd no idea Gertz was involved and thought some gal suffering from cabin-fever had taken a notion for Ned. Then I realized there's a shortage of women in these parts, not men, and who'd have him when there's a choice?'

'So how did you find out it was Gertz who was ordering him about?'

'Ned always bragged to me about the extra money he was earning running errands for Gertz.'

'Your brother knew my pa didn't own our farm outright. How come?'

'From Gertz. He said it in passing, sitting right where you are. I was there. He was laughing his head off as we could see your pa struggling with some wood over at the saloon — all that effort just to make up the payments. Got up and went over and kicked hell out of him. Made me sick. Barred him from this place. I knew your pa in the old times.'

'In Tennessee?'

'Naw. We came from there originally, but my folks left there when I was no more than a kid. From the old days in Flat Stone. Your pa was quiet and dignified in the old days and could've put Gertz in the ground quite easily if he'd had a mind to.'

'So why didn't he?'

But Kaid already knew the answer. Gertz wasn't the guy Pa was waiting for. Annie's voice brought his mind back to the present.

'When I saw your pa waving that knife about, it was like I was seeing the clock turned back fifteen years. The spirit was there again and he was ready to take on the world. Came in here and told me to look after the folks on the rise. Make sure they were remembered, and then he was gone.'

'Had he been in a fight?'

'Nope. Nor was he off his head. Cool and clear, that was his thinking, hand holding the knife as steady as a rock. His eyes were wild but they always were in the old days.'

'What old days, Annie?'

'When your family first came to Flat Stone, before I left to seek my fortune.' Annie smiled at the thought. 'Loads of laughs then with you and him when you would come into town. Adored him, you did when you were hardly any size at all. He'd be right proud to think you cared enough to avenge him but would probably tell me to stop you wasting any more of your life.'

'Did he come in here of a Sunday?'

'Never. But I took him over some soup and bread and coffee whether he wanted it or not. Just left it round the back. He was a proud man and he was embarrassed by a woman seeing him humiliated so much.'

'By Gertz?'

Annie nodded and a terrible sadness invaded her dark eyes. 'Don't you go looking him up! Gertz is a dangerous man.'

'Have to, Annie, for two reasons. The second is he knows who did that to Pa, and the first is my pa ain't dead.'

9

Darkness had fallen and Kaid had the distinct feeling as he headed for the saloon that he was being watched. His senses were on full alert but the lights from the windows of the buildings lining the street were sufficient only to throw their shadows all around.

'Kaid!' The sudden whisper from no more than an arm's length away nearly scared the hell out of him and he knew he should have let his hand draw the gun. Kaid McEntyre was still a farm boy. If he continued like this he'd also be a dead one.

'Jude, you stupid sonofabitch. Don't do that again!' He quickly pushed the boy further into the blackness of the alley away from prying eyes. 'I told you to stay put. Door shut, mouth in the same position.'

'Got some information.'

'OK. Spit it out.' The moon was emerging from behind the thunderclouds and Jude's anxiety was clearly etched on his face. 'Ain't you got any kin who might be worrying about you?'

'Naw. It's Gertz.'

'That's where I'm heading right now.'

'Thought as much. Well, he ain't in the saloon.'

'I told you to stay safe.'

'I did. Saw him ride out hard along the Decault Road right after you left and he ain't come back as far as I know. I reckon he might be heading for the farm.'

'Checking up.'

'On the sheriff?' Jude suggested.

'On Pa, I guess. Just makin' sure.' A slow smile gradually transformed Kaid's normally stern face. 'Even if Gertz finds out my pa's still alive, it's too late to inform his boss, for you know what, kid? My guess is that that guy's already on the move. In fact he's probably here in Flat Stone right now, waiting for the nod from Gertz. I just have to wait for Gertz to make contact, then I'll make damned sure that guy never sees our farm, or anything else, again.' Jude jammed himself against the clapboard wall intent on disappearing from sight. 'Relax. He thinks Pa's dead and whatever it was between them is dead along with him. Thinks he's safe. Just maybe wants to head on out there and gloat. The only other person who knows what it's all about is the mountain man. I reckon that hunter's set on killing him as well as my pa, but that guy doesn't realize that yet — and it's all to do with Tennessee.'

'But why?'

'Don't know, don't care. I'll kill them both if I have to.'

'Ain't possible to talk a man to death, Kaid.' Jude had a nasty habit of stating the obvious.

'I've got it all figured out,' said Kaid, trying to reassure both Jude and himself.

'You're a liar and I'm moving away from you as fast as I can. I'm as likely to be killed by a bullet from your gun as anybody else's.'

'Get back home. Stay indoors and keep the bolts on till you hear me tell you it's all over.'

'This is a peaceful town, Kaid.'

'I know. I've seen the handbills. Come to Flat Stone Creek. Opportunities for all. Go West, young man. Don't mention one preacher and one sheriff dead and my pa near dead all in a matter of hours.'

'Kaid, I was helping the preacher that night his buggy was bust carry some stuff from the Doyle spread for the collation when we were overtaken by Mr Rattigan and some of his boys just outside town. For some reason the reverend was really shaken by it, I could tell.'

'I thought Mr Rattigan had never been to Flat Stone? How did you know it was him?'

'Sneaking around this town day and night is my business. Knowledge is power.' Jude had read that somewhere but right then he couldn't figure out where. 'Heard Walt Gertz call him by his name once in the office back of the saloon. Seems he sometimes came in after the town was all closed up. Liked his privacy, he told Gertz.' Even more to think about and Kaid didn't have the time.

'Anyway, do like I say, Jude, and stay low.' Kaid watched as the boy slunk away avoiding Main Street. With no Gertz around, he reckoned his best bet was the mountain men. They were the other main danger to Pa and time was running out. He had a gut feeling they would make their move soon. If they were still in Flat Stone, they'd be in Rattigan's and at least he wouldn't have to get past Gertz. Keeping well into the shadows, he made for the saloon. Flat Stone was small but noisy and busy during the day, but at night the saloons vied with the eating-houses for bucks burning holes in the never-ending procession of ranch hands' pockets. Intermittent pools of yellow light broke the darkness, cascading over the dusty street, pinpointing accurately the laughter and music that accompanied men at play. Annie's was full and doing a roaring trade and Rattigan's eerily echoing piano was almost in tune as Kaid breasted the batwings. If the McEntyres had been local news for the past few days, they weren't any longer and nobody paid him any heed. Walt Gertz was missing, as expected, but the hunters were in the same corner as last time, a half-empty bottle and five whiskey glasses, liquid barely touched, bearing witness to the fact that the mountain men liked to do their real drinking back at their camp. They were there — waiting. For whom and for what? The youngest one was missing as always and their easy bearing belied the fact that they were poised and ready for trouble. It suddenly came to him from way back that theirs was an attitude familiar to him as a kid on the trail to Flat Stone. Kaid McEntyre now saw his pa in them.

'You drink or you're out, son.' The barkeep was a disciple of Gertz's school of hospitality.

'I'm drinking with them.' The barkeep followed his gaze and thought better of challenging the four guys who looked like they could fell a bear with one collective spit. Kaid walked over to their table.

'You ain't drinking with us, son, so beat it.'

'I can pay my own way — if and when I want a drink.' The one who had spoken eyed Kaid, took in the worn outfit and expensive gun and holster but said nothing more. Their buckskin outfits all differed in every way from each other but all were designed to blend into their surroundings, and in that saloon they certainly did that. It was the wariness in their eyes that set them apart, their way of holding themselves as if coiled to pounce. Yet, overall, they seemed to the casual glance like four men relaxed and comfortable in each others' company. Kaid eyed up the glasses and bottle and knew not a sip of whiskey had crossed their lips and wouldn't till the job was done.

'Came to have a word with Walt Gertz but he ain't here.'

The oldest mountain man who seemed to be their spokesman just smiled slowly at Kaid.

'So?'

'So I decided to have a word with you guys instead.'

'We're busy.'

'I can see that.' They were prepared for trouble, that much was obvious to Kaid.

'Good, so beat it.'

'Expecting trouble?'

'We're mountain men. Always trouble of some kind up there.'

'But right now you're in Flat Stone Creek.'

'Old habits die hard but some keep you alive. Now, son, you've had your word. Go back to the farm and make sure the only body the posse took was the sheriff's.'

'I don't reckon your sidekick would let them touch my pa. Reckons he's his quarry.'

'Right and wrong, son; you're right and wrong at the same time. Now just stay clear and let the big boys sort this one out.'

'It's all McEntyre business and I aim to be right there when it's sorted out.'

'That statement tells me you're a lad of principle and a complete fool. Either one would get you shot. I've warned you. That's as much as I can do. You get in the way, you'll be taken out faster than you can blink, and with no regrets.'

'I know how to use this.' The mountain man nodded and looked appreciatively at the Peacemaker.

'Oh yeah, the badge. We heard. Which one were you really aiming for? Don't be a fool, son. There's a big wide world out there. Saddle up and enter it. Leave this god-forsaken hole and live.'

'Not without my pa.'

'Then you'd better pick your spot on

that rise, for when he leaves he'll be horizontal and in a pine box. Now don't try anything foolish right now for there's four of us in front of you and Nathan right behind you.' Kaid spun round and looked into the dark-blue eyes of Nathan Chesney.

'That's sound advice you've been given by Lucas. You should seriously consider taking it.' It was the third time Kaid had heard him speak and the soft baritone somehow held the same dire threat as his rifle had. 'Don't even think about it.'

Kaid's first reaction had been to save Pa right then and it had been anticipated by Nathan Chesney. Kaid felt himself a useless apology of a man.

'You got the right sentiments, son, but the wrong upbringing.' The oldest man, Lucas, spoke again as Nathan Chesney eased his lean body out of a side door after an exchange of words with him and was gone. 'You just be careful with that gun. No grandstanding. Any of these here guys, Ethan,

229

Johnny and Harry, get hit by a bullet from that Peacemaker, intentionally or otherwise, and I'll personally rip your head off with my bare hands. Keep it holstered at all times unless you aim to shoot yourself — and you'd better do that in a riverbed miles from civilization so as to keep the population safe.'

'I aim to stop Chesney killing my pa and find out who beat him up.'

'Then you're going in two directions at the same time. Mind you, for a McEntyre, that ain't so difficult. Nathan will kill your pa no matter what, so don't kick against a brick wall. It's a long story and it's his right. Accept it.'

Kaid stayed exactly where he was. Nathan Chesney had gone and he'd no idea where. What Kaid couldn't figure out was why they were in Flat Stone and not at their camp. What were they all waiting for?

'I wasn't brought up to quit.'

'That don't surprise me.' It didn't surprise him because he knew all the answers and Kaid, whose family was involved, didn't even know the questions. It was time he got the hell out of there, for he was beginning to get the impression he was being kept talking for a purpose. This mountain man was doing something everybody knew never happened in his circles when off the mountains — uttering more than two sentences every hour. Where was Nathan Chesney now?

'Did you know my pa way back?' But the hunter was through talking. And now the mountain man's eyes were no longer wary but alert. Kaid turned slowly and watched as Gertz now stood by the batwings, the other customers suddenly finding they had appointments elsewhere. His eyes were firmly fixed on Kaid.

'You bothering these guys?'

'He was just leaving.' Kaid heard the mountain man's quiet voice.

'Yeah, just passing the time of day. Guess I'll have a drink before I go.' Kaid's voice sounded hollow in his ears.

'The bar's closed.' Gertz's sidekick

had appeared from the backroom and his announcement was backed up by the barkeep, who scrawled the same on a blackboard above the bar.

'That go for you too, Walt? Gets mighty thirsty riding around these parts on your own,' added Kaid.

'The all-seeing McEntyres. Pity your pa didn't see who beat him up. Maybe the new sheriff will have more luck — your pa still being alive and well.' That was welcome news to Kaid.

'Pa saw who it was all right, and I got a gut feeling it was one of the good old Tennessee boys.'

'Is that right? Now, on your way.'

'Seems like everybody's telling me to leave Flat Stone. But I guess that isn't what you're suggesting, is it?'

'You tell me.' Gertz's man lolled carelessly against the bar as Gertz poured himself a drink. 'These glasses ain't clean,' he complained as the whiskey hit the bottom of the one nearest him.

'Could get you closed down — just a

complaint or two in the right ear and, let's face it, you're no Mr Tom Rattigan. No influence where it counts.' He turned his attention back to Kaid.

'Guess way out on that farm with no more than dust and a senile old guy for company could make a farm boy talk too much when he meets other folks. Minding your own business could just keep you living that little bit longer. It's a lesson you'd better learn fast.'

The hunters just sat watching. It wasn't their argument and Kaid was now out on his own with the man who'd virtually called the shots in Flat Stone for as long as he could remember.

'What was it that you were promised when you'd seen to Pa and the preacher?' Gertz's face changed. 'Maybe I should pay Mr Rattigan a visit next time he tears himself away from the capital to visit his ranch and let him know what you get up to.'

'Why not?' Almost immediately Kaid felt himself freeze as the ear-splitting blast of a gun being fired close by

233

exploded in his head. A second had passed, that was all, and yet a man lay dead, slumped beside the polished mahogany of the bar, a hunting knife deeply embedded in his chest.

'You can clean him out along with the glasses,' observed Gertz.

Kaid watched mesmerized as the mountain man pulled the hunting knife out of Gertz's sidekick's body and cleaned it on the bar towel. The one called Lucas kicked the Navy Colt that had almost deafened Kaid to the opposite side of the room before turning to Kaid. He pointed to Gertz's still holstered Peacemaker and smiled as he spoke. 'Wise move. Consider yourself a very lucky man, Gertz. It would seem there's some sense in paying another man to make your mistakes for you.'

'Is someone hurt?' Kaid recognized the preacher's widow's voice as the mountain men roughly hauled the dead man behind the counter.

'No, ma'am, just dead.' The hunter

sheathed his knife as she entered the now-silent saloon, her eyes fixed firmly on Kaid. He had the feeling she'd been there for some time and her next words proved it.

'My guess, Kaid, is you'd be better off staying in here. Plenty of company.' She meant witnesses and her implication wasn't lost on Gertz either. 'Mind you, it looks like the barman has quit too.' The bar was now deserted except for the unseen body behind it. 'They say your pa's dead, son. Doesn't seem to stop, does it? My husband worked all his life to bring some sort of order to this place, order and a bit of decency.' Her eyes narrowed slightly as they rested on Gertz. She was wasting everybody's time but he was now quite happy for her to do so. The missing barkeep, Kaid supposed, would be hot-footing it to the jailhouse, hoping there'd be enough lawmen there to arrive back at the saloon in time to keep Gertz from getting himself killed. He'd keep her talking as long as he could.

'A McEntyre's been involved in all of them, Mrs McWilliams,' said Gertz silkily. 'No idea how to behave once they're off that dirt farm. God knows how they were brought up.'

Kaid's fist smacked off Gertz's jaw almost simultaneously with the sound of the last word spoken. But Gertz lashed back fast and sent Kaid sprawling against the nearest table. 'Mind your manners in front of ladies.'

Kaid had a lot to learn and he knew it. His lip was split but so was Gertz's cheek. He could almost see without looking the expression of exasperation that would be on the mountain man's face. 'Now, ma'am, don't see as how we can be of any help to you, this being a saloon and all.'

'My business is with Kaid McEntyre, Mr Gertz, but it's not especially private. Well, not any more, it isn't.' The woman turned to Kaid as she spoke, her hands clasped in front of her. 'I've been thinking — about that night — when Ben came back late looking very flustered.' Kaid kept quiet about Jude's being there and hoped the preacher's widow would too.

'Remembered anything?'

'No, nothing to remember, for my husband said very little.' Gertz relaxed visibly despite the loud peal of thunder that ripped through the air. 'Ben was a meticulous man, though. Always kept records. He liked to make little notes as well in his journal. Made some that night. Maybe you'd care to come over some time and have a look.'

Kaid nodded. 'Be happy to see the book, ma'am.'

Mrs McWilliams smiled and nodded towards the mountain men. 'These your pa's friends?' She seemed so vulnerable, Kaid forced himself to nod. Mrs McWilliams stopped just inside the batwings. 'You see, Kaid, from what he wrote that night in his book, it seems to imply that your pa just ain't your pa — your real one.' The woman shrugged and looked worn out with grief. 'I've left it for you on the bench by the meeting house. I think you should read it.'

Kaid stared at the empty doorway once she'd gone and then a glance at the mountain men confirmed that they'd known all along. Kaid's legs suddenly buckled under him as a bullet tore straight through his side. The barman's body whipped backwards and splattered off the piano as the mountain man's gunshots found his head and chest four times in quick succession. The piano went tunelessly berserk as the barman's finger jerked convulsively time and time again against the trigger of his gun and sprayed the ivories beyond repair.

'Thought he'd legged it. Why the hell did he go for McEntyre leaving any one of us who can shoot to take him out without breaking sweat?' Kaid heard the other mountain men speak for the first time.

'Guess he didn't leave after all. Big mistake on his part.'

'Ain't met a barman yet with any savvy.'

'Well, it's too late for this one to learn any, Johnny. Haul him back there beside his sidekick, and Harry, for God's sake shut that piano lid.' A quick look round told them that Gertz had gone.

'Has he left town?' Kaid wanted Gertz real bad. He wanted to squeeze every last bit of information out of him, wanted so badly to come face to face with the man who'd hurt his pa, the only pa he'd known. What the preacher's widow had said just didn't make sense.

'Nope. He knows Nathan's out there so he'll be skulking among the shadows. Ethan, take a look at the kid's side. Looks to me like that holster of his took the brunt.'

'Aw, for God's sake! It ain't mine. It's Mr Grant's and he waited six months for this. It's bespoke and now look at the state it's in.' That was all Kaid could muster as the blood was quickly wiped away with expert ease and no little amount of pain.

'Vanity,' pronounced the one called Harry. 'When the hell's a blacksmith gonna wear a holster like that?'

'Flesh ripped clear away, Lucas. It's nothing.' A torn bit of bar towel was quickly packed into the hole and the wound was forgotten. The mountain men were in a huddle and plans were being made.

'This is my fight — mine,' Kaid hissed between clenched teeth.

'No it ain't, son. It's Nathan's. So you leave it to him.'

'Oh no, it's my family, my fight.'

'The widow just told you Jerem ain't your pa.'

'He brought me and the children up for a lifetime. That makes him my pa.'

The hunter looked at him long and hard before speaking again. 'OK, where do you aim to start?'

'Find Gertz.'

'And where are you gonna look? There are a hundred shadows out there and he could be in any one of them. Gertz would gun you down in a minute and you'd never even know he was there. To find Gertz, you need hunters and that's us. You do as we say, and we'll get him.'

'Do you reckon he killed the preacher?'

'Didn't deny it.' A sudden realization hit them all at the same time.

'Mrs McWilliams was out there all the time. She heard. What the hell did all that mean about Pa and the book?'

'Means the preacher's widow's a better hunter than you, son.' The mountain men all moved past him like wraiths, no sound at all now emanating from those men. Kaid tried his best to keep up but they'd fanned out and vanished within seconds. What had she meant: his pa wasn't his pa? But he had to think and think fast. A hunter, they'd said of her, and a hunter laid traps. His side was burning up but he had to stop her, had to help her. The meeting house and the book. Of course, both said to lure Gertz there. He shuffled on his way across Main Street as silently as he could, waiting for the sound of gunfire, eternally grateful that he heard none. They'd been wrong, all of them.

Relief swept over him as he silently entered the back yard and saw Mrs McWilliams casually leaning against the well. Four other figures stood by her, the slanting beams of a spring moon illuminating Gertz's inert body, his head smashed to gory pieces beneath an ancient stone quern.

'I reckon it's time Gertz left town again.' Lucas's suggestion was evidently accepted and the preacher's buggy lurched as Gertz, along with the earth on which his brains had splattered and the avenging stone, were put on board after they'd put the horse between the shafts. Disused mines were plentiful among the foothills and nobody round these parts was foolish enough to climb down dangerous shafts. 'Nosy sonofabitch fell down a mine and called time on his life here on earth. Chuck the stone down a different one. Won't take more than an hour, Johnny, at the most, and any rain will keep folks indoors once it starts. Bring the buggy back here and then head on out to the dirt farm on Kaid's horse. It's over there at the blacksmith's place, right?

Kaid nodded in agreement.

'Kaid'll take yours. We don't want him going over there right now. Best we stay back here in the shadows.' Lucas walked over to the widow and spoke in a gentle voice to her. 'Now, ma'am, an eye for an eye as the Good Book says, so think no more of it. Was about to put a bullet in him myself.'

'He murdered poor Ben. Why?'

'I think the answer's in that book you left on the bench, ma'am.' Kaid answered her question.

She was still leaning against the well as the buggy pulled away. She shook her head. 'It doesn't make any sense.'

'About my pa, Mrs McWilliams.'

'The book itself will tell you nothing more than what I said. Doesn't name names. I saw you go into the saloon and all I wanted to know was whether you'd learned anything about my husband's death. That's when I heard you all talking. Are you hurt, Kaid? Let me help you. Come inside.'

'I haven't got time, ma'am. Somebody wants my pa dead.' Kaid glanced at the hunters and knew at last what it was all about. Nathan Chesney was after his pa all right, but not the pa who'd raised him. But Mrs McWilliams was speaking once more.

'The book records the marriage of your ma and Jerem McEntyre. They were cousins. Ben said all that family married cousins.'

'When did he tell you that?'

'That morning you came round to speak to him. He was confused. Couldn't make head nor tail of it all. He'd seen a man on the road the night before riding along with another group of men protecting him — a man from Tennessee he'd assumed had been dead for more than fifteen years.'

'Did he say who he was?'

'No, just kept thumbing through the

book as if it would speak to him and clear his mind. All the time he was saying, 'I thought he must have died and she'd married another McEntyre back in Tennessee where they'd come from.' There were dozens of them, it seems, all called after the old grandfather.' The truth began its long and tortuous journey through Kaid's mind.

'You should go indoors, ma'am,' advised Lucas, 'and I guess you'd best keep the reverend's book, too.' The preacher's house was just a few steps from the meeting house. One of the men peeled off and led her to home and family.

'She'll tell what she did, Lucas.'

'And who'll believe her, Ethan? You heard her. A fragile woman getting the better of Gertz. They'll think she's lost her mind for a bit with grief. Two dead in the saloon and Gertz missing. A falling out of thieves.'

'What about his horse?'

'It ain't outside the saloon. Could have left it anywhere. Obviously up to no good.' But Kaid interrupted them. 'Nathan Chesney's after my real pa. He knows who he is and so do you.'

The mountain man shook his head. 'We know who he is but not what he looks like.'

'If Nathan had known that, he'd have put a bullet in him years ago.'

'Why is he after him?'

'Because he systematically destroyed Nathan's pa's life.'

'Nathan Chesney. So Nathan's Pa's son. Pa wasn't warning me about him. He was wanting me to fetch him, fetch his son.'

'In an odd sort of way, Jerem McEntyre Chesney's a very lucky man. He's got two sons looking out for him. Now, Kaid, watch and learn and don't move till you get the nod from me. That way we all know where we stand. That way we can see each other. You're about to get your first lesson in hunting and it's all about patience. We wait.'

'Where?'

'Near Rattigan's saloon.'

'Who for?'

'An educated guess says the preacher saw your other pa on the road that night. The only guy who visits the saloon at night surrounded by his men and nobody ever sees him is Rattigan himself.' Kaid's shocked mind refused to take it all in. 'It's hard to bear, Kaid, but now ain't the time to get emotional.'

'Jude said it was Mr Rattigan,' said Kaid. 'Jude was helping the Reverend McWilliams out that night and saw him.'

Lucas nodded. 'The preacher was probably trying to see him for an explanation. Asking for a meeting through Gertz got him killed. We're gonna wait for the real Jerem McEntyre alias Tom Rattigan to show up and let Nathan Chesney avenge his pa if Jerem ain't up to it, for Rattigan has robbed Jerem Chesney of sixteen years of his life and a son he loved dearly.'

10

'D'you reckon he's out there now, Lucas?' asked Kaid.

'No doubt about it. We've got him covered. We think he's that guy down by the blacksmith's — watching and listening. Nathan spotted him a while ago.'

'Think he knows about Gertz?' Kaid was worried.

'Nope, for he's only hearing what we want him to hear. Every time he tries to move out, Nathan hems him in — not that he realizes it. Nathan spotted Gertz sneaking up to the saloon.' Lucas watched the street intently as he spoke.

'Was that what he came to let you know?'

'Yeah, probably wanting that drink before linking up with Rattigan.'

'What makes you so positive that it might be him?' Kaid asked.

'Rattigan doesn't yet know for sure whether your pa's dead. Gertz hadn't got in touch with him, according to Nathan, so he's still in the dark and waiting for the word. He'll find that out when it suits us. Problem is none of us knows what he looks like except your pa. We'll only be guessing and having to wait until he makes his move kinda gives Rattigan the edge. There's no way we want him out at the farm before we get there if we can possibly help it. The minute your pa's back on his feet he'll be in action again, and there's no better hunter ever lived.'

Kaid reluctantly spoke again, 'The kid who helps out at the blacksmith's knows Rattigan.'

The hunter shook his head decisively. 'Don't want to involve a kid. Likely to get himself killed. A showdown with McEntyre's what Jerem wanted and we aim to give it to him. He won't want anybody else getting hurt.'

'What about Nathan's right?' Kaid was scared for his pa.

'Same thing. Pa and son. They always worked together when Nathan was a kid. About time they got together again.'

But there was no way Kaid was going to allow himself to be locked out of this. 'He's my pa, too. Sixteen years of slaving side by side makes him that. All Rattigan did was hold us like slaves on that land.'

'And you want Jerem to survive this?'

'Sure, you know that.'

'Then do as I say — exactly as I say.' Pa was no longer the quarry, no longer the victim. Tom Rattigan didn't yet know it but he was now being hunted down and there would only be one outcome. Kaid felt nothing but hatred for the man who'd treated his family so badly, but his fear was that good men would be taken out along with him. He wasn't worth Pa or Nathan or any of the mountain men. But there was no way Pa would get on with his life without avenging his family.

'I'll do that,' agreed Kaid.

'He thinks Jerem's dead but he ain't absolutely sure of it.'

'Is Nathan back there?' asked Kaid. 'Is he still watching Rattigan or the guy we think is Rattigan?' Right then Kaid realized that Nathan had enough discipline and respect for his pa to wait his turn. If Pa failed, Nathan would do it for him.

'Don't matter to you where Nathan is. All we have to do is lure Rattigan back there tonight so that this whole matter can be settled for good. Now we have to make sure we even up the sides, for Jerem ain't quite fit. He won't want any favours but on a level ground, Rattigan doesn't stand a chance. If you've got mixed feelings, son, you'd best stay well out of it. There's no room for that and it could just get some friends killed. We'd all understand. No hard feelings.'

'I'm with Pa.'

'Then right now we need to get that saloon back in business so that Rattigan thinks everything is fine.'

'I'll get Annie — she's an old friend of Pa's — to see to it. That place'll be jumping in five minutes. Only the piano will be missing and a couple of bodies.'

Lucas nodded. 'Right, Kaid. On your way and then get back here pronto. Use the back alleys.' Kaid didn't wait to be told twice.

Annie's cook shop was oddly quiet, full but subdued as the strange silence emanating from the saloon made the customers wary. Gunshots meant little, but a silent piano was bad news. That was how Rattigan would see it too. Annie was in her office at the back, the door still open, hired help mingling. But this time they let him go right on in. She sat on the edge of the desk, waiting.

'What happened?'

'Bar staff went trigger-happy and Gertz is evidently out of town.'

'There'll be hell to pay when he gets back.' She looked Kaid straight in the eye and a slow, beautiful smile transformed the usually stern face. 'Guess we're running out of guys from Tennessee.'

Kaid nodded. 'I need your help, Annie.'

'To do what?'

'Liven Rattigan's up a bit.'

'A normal night in Flat Stone. I guess some of my boys will have to double up as the bar staff.'

Kaid nodded. 'Now?'

'Right now.' Annie moved like greased lightning and Kaid watched her hired help leave on the double.

'Drinks on the house at Rattigan's for the next ten minutes starting right now!' The cook shop emptied before Annie's words died on the air.

'The piano's bust,' warned Kaid.

Annie laughed. 'Could be an improvement.' Flat Stone's drunks, drifters and general riffraff were still short of a discerning ear amongst their numbers and Kaid heard a few brief attempts at *The Red River Valley* before he left by the back door, Annie now standing thoughtfully by her desk. He rejoined Lucas in the darkened anonymity of the meeting house alley. Everything in Flat Stone sounded normal and he hoped that Rattigan would be convinced.

'Listen, Kaid, Rattigan has come into Flat Stone to see Gertz. Wants to know how the land lies. His aim is to finish off Jerem — if he's still alive — the first opportunity he gets and we're gonna give him it.'

'But why? If he thinks Pa and me are leaving Flat Stone now because we've lost the farm, why bother?'

'He knows your pa won't leave without trying to settle that debt.'

'But he's always known there'd be a chance of that. He could've killed Pa long ago.'

'Rattigan is evil. He wouldn't stop Jerem suffering a minute earlier than he needed to. That was why Jerem made such a commotion the other night. It was all meant to get back to Rattigan and Jerem knew he wouldn't be able to resist coming for him.'

'So that provoked the beating. In the

dark — with Gertz holding Pa?'

'Sounds like his style. Gertz probably took the knife away with him and used it on the preacher. Always was his preferred method, it seems. The miracle is he didn't use it on Jerem. But then again, he probably thought that by the time they'd finished it wasn't necessary.'

'Did Nathan give Pa the knife?'

Lucas nodded. 'Seems he didn't even have a gun. Was gonna use his bare hands. Jerem knew who Rattigan was all the time and only he will be able to explain what he's done and why he did it for all those years.'

'And Pa wouldn't tell Nathan, is that it? Was that what all the threats were about that night? Trying to keep him well out of it?'

'Right. Now as far as Rattigan's concerned, Jerem's dead, but being the vicious swine that he is, he's probably wanting to stand over his grave and laugh. He'll know Gertz rode out courtesy of the late barkeep — and a more loyal employee never breathed, but now he doesn't — and Rattigan is probably waiting for him to return. But we both know he ghosted into Flat Stone and now ain't likely to keep his appointment.'

'And you want to lure Rattigan out to the farm?'

'Who said farm boys had no brains?' Kaid laughed softly as Lucas spoke. 'But this ain't the time to start using them. We need instinct here, Kaid, a hunter's experience and a hunter's instinct.'

'To nudge him into the trap?'

'That's it.'

'Does Pa know?'

'Not the fine details as yet — but he will in good time. That's part of the trap. I know how Jerem works and it's up to me to use that knowledge to keep him alive, for right now he doesn't care if he dies in the attempt to avenge your family. So we'll bring that tiny bit of recklessness into our plan to get him in and out of this in one piece.'

'Rattigan ain't worth my pa's life.'

'I agree, son, but your pa doesn't and that's what we have to work with. If we take Jerem up to the mountains, he'll only come back. We finish it now, Kaid.' Lucas's eyes looked deep into Kaid's soul and Kaid knew he intended keeping him well away from the action.

'You'll let Nathan avenge his pa but you're not letting me,' Kaid accused Lucas.

'Nathan's a hunter, born and raised that way. Besides, nobody should have the blood of his pa, blood father or otherwise, on his hands. You can help justice, not revenge, by doing just like I say. I have to know I can rely on you completely to do as you're told or it won't happen. I'd put a bullet in your leg right now if I thought you were gonna endanger us all by going off half-cocked.'

'Lucas, you can count on me absolutely.'

'Fine. Now we're gonna let Rattigan know your pa's alive. That way he won't wait for Gertz. The temptation to gloat, then kill a sick man will be too great. Is Annie still back there?'

'She's here, Lucas.' Ethan's words were spoken softly and Annie quietly joined them in the alley.

'You knew she'd follow me,' said Kaid.

'Strong-minded women like to know who's giving them orders.' There was admiration in the hunter's voice and Lucas turned to the woman who'd served them stew on many occasions.

'You're looking for Rattigan now, is that it? Gertz's boss?' she asked.

'Have to make sure he gets a certain piece of information but we don't rightly know what he looks like.'

'I know Rattigan. He's from Tennessee, like everybody else it seems. Likes to have Tennessee boys around him, said Ned. That's probably why he put up with my brother. He was no Wyatt Earp,' Annie added sourly before continuing: 'We were from Tennessee too, but my family left when Tom and I were just kids. Never knew him from there. I was just curious one night when I saw the riders arriving after dark at the saloon, so I sorta did a bit of sidling around. Like to keep my finger on Flat Stone's pulse, so to speak. Fell over that kid Jude doing the same thing. What's this all about? Are the chickens coming home to roost at last?'

'A little score to be settled, that's all.' Lucas smiled and knew Annie wasn't fooled.

'Between you and Rattigan?'

'Naw, Rattigan and his cousin from back in Tennessee. We reckon he might be the guy in the shadows over by the blacksmith's.'

Annie nodded, apparently satisfied, and with that she quickly left the alley and walked determinedly back to the cook shop. Lucas suddenly moved fast out of the alley and round the back, disappearing into the deep shadow after her. Kaid was puzzled but he and the others stayed where he knew they could be found by Lucas on his return.

Keeping an eye on the relentless comings and goings in Main Street, they watched as Annie reappeared shortly, carrying a pot, presumably containing the famous Irish stew, and came on down towards them. Lucas joined them once more and watched as she walked all the way down Main Street to the blacksmith's. Her boot kicked off the door as she bellowed for Jude to open it.

'Get this open right now, you lazy good-for-nothing. I've got a cook shop to run.' Another well-aimed kick! Jude was staying put as ordered. 'Open up and take this pot from me before I kick the door down. You'd better have that fire going full blast, for John Grant and the family are on their way back and they'll want some grub and hot at that.' The drifter, who had been squatting near by, sauntered along and Annie glanced at him. 'Would you shoot that bloody lock off, friend, before I break my foot.'

'I'm coming, I'm coming!' Jude's

anxious voice rang from within.

'You'd better be or Ellie and Lizzie will have you strung up by your ears. The lazy kid's been sleeping as usual,' she remarked bitterly to the drifter before shouting once more. 'If this is cold when they get here, you're for it.' Her voice was loud and angry and Jude wasn't hanging about. Kaid prayed that Seb wouldn't hear the commotion and come running from the undertaker's. As the locks rattled Annie stepped back. Glancing at the drifter, she thanked him with a smile. 'Guess the gun won't be needed. Folks getting back to their own beds need comforting food after what they've been putting up with.' She kicked the door again and Jude opened it wide.

'I ain't been sleeping,' Jude protested. 'Is Mr McEntyre dead right enough?'

'Not that scrawny degenerate. Just chucked them out, ungrateful sonofa-bitch. Ellie sent word to bring some decent grub over for John and Seb, for they'll have to work round the clock to make up for lost time. And you too. You can loaf around when you've got money like Tom Rattigan. So move it, son, before they get here.'

She could be heard ordering him about, pots clashing as Jude closed the door, shutting out the yellow glow of the lamps and dimming the receding back of the drifter.

'Got him,' whispered Lucas, his plan hatched with Annie having borne fruit. Kaid and the hunters were now mounted and within minutes were heading fast towards the dirt farm. The drifter slipped into an alley a few buildings further along the street and, in minutes, he too was heading for the farm and Jerem McEntyre Chesney. He didn't have the advantage of being led by his son, for right then, mounted on Johnny's horse, Kaid was leading the mountain men along old tracks that he'd had to walk for sixteen years. The shorter route would give them the time advantage they needed.

The moon was full in a now

cloudless, starlit sky and its beams flooded the land about the farm as the riders rode relentlessly on. Destiny was beckoning and Kaid's stomach was in knots at the thought of losing Pa. The mountain men were silent, each knowing exactly which part he was expected to play in the drama now unfolding and in that lay their strength. Kaid was being marginalized. He knew and understood that but, given half a chance, neither Pa or Nathan would beat him to it. As the dimly lit cabin, a tiny islet in a moonlit sea, came into view, his eyes deliberately rested on the rise with its now unseen crosses. *You're gonna walk away from this, Pa*, he vowed, *and it'll be my gift to you for a lifetime of sacrifice*. Lucas glanced over at him and shook his head. Lucas's instincts were well-honed.

'That ain't gonna happen.' His words were soft but Kaid heard them just the same.

'I'll do as you asked.' Up to a point, but somehow Lucas had always known that, thought Kaid, and Lucas would be ready to step in and make sure Kaid did exactly as he'd been told, no more, no less. They slowed almost to walking pace and Kaid wondered whether Nathan was already with Pa. But he could see no horses on their land.

'What about the Grants?'

'They've gone. Weren't you listening to Annie?' Lucas had primed Annie as to what she should say, but Kaid hadn't thought it through. There was no way there'd be anybody there but themselves. No innocent folks would be allowed to get either hurt or in the way. They wanted it over and done with that night. Rattigan was on his way to finish off what he hadn't managed the last time and Kaid knew he'd never think of that man as anything but Rattigan. He wanted to know why it had all happened, but there was no way Kaid was coming back home that night to talk. Those graves were sending messages to him right then and that was all that was needed. Silent witnesses, but their cries screamed in his head.

They tethered the horses amongst the scrub and dying trees in a dip some distance away from the cabin, their forms mingling with the dappled light as the men stole silently up to it. Rattigan wouldn't ride right in there unless he had to. The only obvious place to hide his horse was behind the rise. He'd want to be in and out fast. But right then, he was way behind them; a familiarity with the land was a gift he'd unknowingly given to his son, which that son was now using to seal Rattigan's own fate and rid his pa of the hatred in his heart for ever. Kaid would do anything now to achieve that for his pa and to get revenge for himself. Kaid McEntyre's legacy from Jerem McEntyre Chesney was honesty and he acknowledged it. He looked into his heart at that moment and saw anger and resentment disappear and a love for his pa grow. There was no way he was going to lose him now.

The cabin wasn't large but the

children had mostly slept in the loft and that was where Ethan was to be positioned, unseen but with a good view of Pa and Rattigan when Pa was stationed at the old oak table. Harry would be somewhere outside, unseen and unheard. They slipped quietly through the back door. Pa was waiting, Nathan had obviously been there and briefed him. The others scattered silently; Harry went back outside to take up watch, and Kaid and Pa were left alone for a moment or two. Kaid stood a few feet away and was glad to see some colour other than that of bruising on his pa's face and a look of rigid determination in his eyes. His day was dawning at last.

'You shouldn't be here, son. Lucas was told to keep you out of it.'

'Nathan has his rights but so have I, Pa.'

Jerem McEntyre Chesney nodded. 'A right not to witness what's going to happen. I owe that to your ma.'

'I don't know exactly what this is all

about but I know you owe nobody round here, living or dead. Not a thing.'

'I'll take care of it and if I don't, Lucas and the boys will. We go way back together. I want you and Nathan away from here.'

'Nathan won't go and you know it.'

'He'll give me my chance. It's how he's been raised. He understands. But you're a boy used to farming — '

'And death,' Kaid cut in. 'Can Nathan equal Sally, Laney, Dave and Ma?'

'His mother — when he was born.' But Kaid shook his head.

'Still gives me the edge on him, Pa.'

'Jerem McEntyre — '

Kaid cut in quickly. 'Jerem McEntyre or Tom Rattigan ain't my pa, their pa or Ma's husband. He's got no right. Never wanted it, by the looks of it, for he owns most of Flat Stone, that ranch in the foothills and God only knows what in the capital. He owns all that and he made damn sure we got the worst land and you got chained to us. How he managed that considering how evil he is and the good man you are, I don't know, but I sure want to.'

'Won't do you any good, Kaid. It's all in the past and tonight will bury it and him for good. I want you out of here. Lucas, get Kaid away from here,' Jerem Chesney called. But Lucas stayed put. 'You know what I said, Lucas, no Nathan, no Kaid. Well, we've not got Nathan here and I won't have Kaid.'

'You ain't salted me away either, Pa.' The voice came from behind Kaid and he was suddenly standing shoulder to shoulder with Nathan Chesney.

'Kaid, Nathan, back here fast!' What signal Lucas heard from Harry, Kaid didn't know but suddenly Jerem Chesney was alone in the kitchen. Kaid watched from the darkened bedroom, saw the dim light from the lamp and the flickering orange flames of the fire dancing up the chimney like frenzied spirits longing to be free. Pa looked relaxed for the first time Kaid could remember; it was the same relaxed attitude of the mountain men he'd seen that first day in the saloon, languid and deceptive, hiding the hard purpose and determination of his mind and body.

There were now five men in that cabin, with Harry outside ready to cut off Rattigan and down him if he attempted to head for his horse. Whether Pa held a gun now Kaid had no way of knowing, for he sat behind the table, his gun hand just off it and, in that light, unseen by anyone entering. But Rattigan would be feeling confident. He'd effected the beating, knew Pa would take time to recover from it and Pa hadn't had that luxury. More than the mountain men and Pa wanted it finished that night.

Suddenly, Rattigan was inside the room, gun in hand, before Kaid realized it. Pa never flinched. He knew Rattigan, knew he'd string out the agony. Jerem Chesney looked up slowly as Rattigan spoke his name in a sneering way. Kaid was looking at his father for the first time he could remember. No memories stirred, no laughter, no singing, no *Buffalo gal won't you come out Tonight* and Kaid thanked God for that. His gun remained holstered on Lucas's orders and he knew Pa was waiting — for what?

'Jerem Chesney! Been a while — well, a short while, OK, but a while since we talked.'

'Don't recall we ever did much of that, cousin. You talked, everybody listened.'

'That was because I was the only guy in that part of Tennessee had anything worth saying.' Rattigan laughed.

'The ladies sure thought so.'

'And Janey believed it all.' Kaid flinched at his mother's name and suddenly realized what his pa was doing. Kaid had a right to know it all but Jerem McEntyre Chesney wouldn't say, didn't have to for he knew Tom Rattigan was a loud-mouth he could lead on.

'Why did you do it? Why bring Janey and the children halfway here and then abandon them? You should have left them back with their kin in Tennessee. It would have been kinder.'

Rattigan shrugged. 'Suddenly saw a chance one day on the trail and took it. Heard you showed up down from Fort Penge and brought them out here to the dirt farm.'

'To you — only you never showed up.'

'Didn't reckon, though, that you'd be fool enough to stay with them. The West's a place for men with no ties and with you acting as pa, that left me free as a bird. Besides, I gave them this place, didn't I?'

'Made them all slave to buy impoverished land from their own father. Saddled them with a mortgage this land couldn't support while you kept the best parcel of land in the foothills. Ain't a natural thing for a father to do.'

'Ancient history. Jerem McEntyre Chesney. The great hunter and family legend. Nobody could equal you in the old man's eyes. Well, in everybody's eyes round Flat Stone; you're nothing but a loser, Jerem. Laughed myself stupid every time Gertz handed me your wages. Janey even persuaded you to drop the Chesney name to save her face. Living with a guy she wasn't married to and her a churchgoer.' Rattigan laughed loud and long. Jerem Chesney's face was deeply pale, his voice a little unsteady as he ignored those comments, pushing on, determined to see it through whatever it cost him.

'You watched them die. Your own children.'

'Lots of kids die out here. Watched you die too, year after year. Can't tell you how much that meant to me. Well, I messed up last time but I won't tonight.' Rattigan held his gun, aiming it straight at Jerem Chesney.

'How could you stomach it, Jerem? How could you watch your own family die and do nothing for them?'

'Her children. Downtrodden, no spunk, just like squawking Janey, who gave you a helluva life. Made me like her a little in the end when I heard that.'

'She was devoted to you. Reckoned you'd come back for them all one day. She had to be here for you no matter what.'

'You should have walked away.' Rattigan had an answer for everything.

'Would have been real easy leaving a woman and four children on their own, to fend for themselves out here. But you know all about that.'

'And that ain't you. Always did allow yourself to be distracted by a pretty face.'

'So what are you here for, Jerem, or is it Tom?'

'Jerem McIntyre's a loser's name so it had better be Tom Rattigan. I'm here to finish the job.'

'What about Kaid?'

Rattigan shrugged. 'Old enough to make his own way. So any last questions, Jerem? Like who's gonna bury you now that you've stupidly sent

273

the Grants away.' Kaid made to move but Lucas held him back in an iron grip, Kaid's pa was talking again.

'Don't figure on dying in this god-forsaken spot.'

'Forgot that. You're a mountain man. Just your bad luck you ran across Janey when you came down to trade. Like I said, Jerem, you're a loser. Guess I could let your body rot right here. It's my land, as you so rightly said, so I could put up the 'Keep Out' notices till you're nothing but dried bones. Maybe even get some mountain men to take them back up to the Sephinas and scatter them to the four winds.' Kaid saw a slight stiffening of Pa's shoulders. Suddenly Rattigan's gun came up but Pa fired first and was speaking once more. 'We ain't done yet, cousin.'

The blood trickled down Rattigan's arm and his gun hand hung useless, his gun still skidding along the floor as Pa spoke again, his voice thick with emotion.

'Keep them back there, Lucas!'

Rattigan's eyes were bright with fear as he backed towards the door. Now Pa was speaking again, mercilessly dinning his loathing of a lifetime into Rattigan's brain.

'You're trash, always have been, but I ain't taking the risk that one day I'll see a look in Kaid's eyes that tells me he's thinking about the time I killed his father, for he's a decent boy and that's how decent folks think.' Rattigan edged out the door.

'Let him go, Harry!' Lucas's voice echoed loud and clear as the sound of Rattigan's boots scrunching fast over the gritty ground came to them and Kaid knew that it was all over. Jerem McEntyre slumped once more in his chair, his energy now spent.

'Sorry you had to hear that, Kaid.'

'Not all of it's been said, Pa.'

'Maybe some day.'

'That's all right by me.'

Lucas once again took control. 'Guess we should eat once Harry sees Rattigan off the premises. He won't be back but we'll watch just the same.' His words were cut short as gunshots rang out nearby and the mountain men vanished quickly into the night. Moonlight drifted languidly along the silent valley where all other movement seemed momentarily suspended, the men etched starkly against the walls of the now empty cabin. Harry's voice suddenly shattered the still night.

'Never saw her, Lucas. She came from back of the rise.' Harry's gun was drawn but not aimed at Annie. 'God knows where she's left her horse.'

'She knew where we were headed the minute she saw Kaid with us back there.' Lucas's voice held a tinge of regret as he spoke. 'You were never going to hear or see her. Guess she's got mountain blood in her.' Lucas walked on over to Annie as she stood etched on the rise, the moonlight illuminating her as she stood over Rattigan's dead body. Kaid nodded to Nathan.

'Let's go bury the real Jerem

McEntyre for good.' Rattigan had fallen partly inside the grave Kaid had dug on that morning when Gorman had appeared. They placed him in it and kicked the red dust deep over him. Kaid looked up as his pa approached slowly.

'It's what Ma always wanted, it seems, to be with him, wasn't it? She was the one who kept us here, not you.'

Jerem Chesney nodded. 'It was what she wanted right enough.'

'Well, she's finally got it.' There was no bitterness in Kaid's voice. It was all over. 'Ma and Pa, RIP.' He pushed the marker into the ground 'You've got a life to lead, Pa. The McEntyres took it away and now I'm giving it back to you. We'd better get Annie and Rattigan's horse back to town.' Annie was just standing and watching, Lucas right by her, holding her gun. She smiled as she spoke.

'Ned was a pathetic apology for a man but he was my brother and he was used by Rattigan just like all the others. I ain't got no kin left now.'

'Harry and Ethan will see you home safely, Annie,' said Lucas softly. 'See you next time we come down to trade.' Annie's eyes washed appreciatively over the hunter. She turned to look long and hard at Jerem Chesney before mounting her horse, which Harry had brought from behind the rise.

'Seems we both have a future worth planning now the bad times are finished. Take care of yourself, Jerem.' With that, she swung her horse round and set off down the trail, Ethan by her side and Harry leading Rattigan's horse, all following the old trail back to Flat Stone.

'Nathan, Kaid, guess you two boys should fetch the Grants back.'

'They'll be back in Flat Stone by now, Lucas,' said Kaid.

'Not a chance, Kaid,' said Jerem. 'Something not quite right with the buckboard. John Grant reckoned it might take a while to fix.'

'In the dark?'

Jerem Chesney smiled as he answered

Kaid. 'Maybe it was nothing after all. That drifter obviously didn't stop to help. We had to make sure Rattigan was convinced it was all genuine. Mrs Grant's belongings are piled up in the loft and you'd better let her take care of that wound.'

'Guess we won't be eating Ethan's beans and jerky tonight with Mrs Grant around,' said Harry.

'Got a feeling Lizzie'll be in a show-off mood tonight,' said Kaid. 'Hope none of you boys, though, are from Indiana.' Kaid laughed at the thought.

11

The old oak table groaned under the weight of food and elbows the next morning as Mrs Grant cooked up a storm.

'Must owe you a small fortune, Ellie, for all this.' Jerem Chesney ate like it was the last meal he'd have on earth.

'Seeing you all eat and laugh here is payment enough. Never was one for picky eaters or a quiet house.'

'First meal I've had in years that didn't have red dust in it.' Kaid had slept little but now felt relaxed and refreshed in spite of it. The dirt farm was quiet outside like always; inside life had begun again.

'A word.' Kaid came out of his reverie as Nathan beckoned in the direction of the door. He followed him out into the yard and sat beside him on the worn steps. 'I didn't mean you any harm. Just tried to warn you off for your own good. Couldn't let you get in too deep or you could've got us all killed.'

'Yeah, Nathan, I understand. No hard feelings. I thought I'd lost everything and was prepared to hate the entire human race.'

'Just as well Pa didn't teach you how to hunt.'

Kaid laughed. 'The mountain men did a good job on you.' Nathan had had no pa for sixteen years and yet he'd understood what Jerem Chesney had been doing. Kaid supposed that was the Chesney strain. The McEntyre one was riddled with selfishness. 'You got Chesney blood all right, Nathan.'

'You got it too, for we've got the same grandpa.'

Kaid felt there was hope then. 'Did Pa always see you when you came down to trade?'

Nathan nodded. 'It was hard at first. Couldn't understand why he hadn't come back home. When he explained it all and I saw the children, I could see how he was trapped — something only a hunter would understand. I swore I'd kill that guy as soon as Pa was free but he wouldn't let me do it. Warned me off that night. Said he'd lost one son that day and didn't want to lose the only other one he had.'

'He threatened you with the knife.'

'He never threatened a youngster in his life. I'd met him back of the saloon. He'd no weapons. I made him take the knife. It just happened to be in his hand later as he warned me off touching Rattigan. It had to be him — had to be Pa himself avenging all of you.'

'Got beaten to it, though.'

'He never could deny a woman anything by all accounts, but on this occasion he didn't know one was there.' There was the sound of footsteps behind them and Jerem Chesney emerged into the heat of the day. The bruising was subsiding and as Kaid looked at his pa he wondered how he'd ever considered him old, for freedom had been given back to him and the life force surged again. His laughter still rang out at something the others had said inside and it was a sound that brought memories flooding back to Kaid, great ones, and he laughed too.

'You owe my pa for that spoiled holster.' Lizzie carelessly tossed the soapy water into the dust as she spoke. 'You ain't thinking of abandoning those hens and chickens, are you?'

'They're for Jude, with thanks. He can start with hens and in no time he'll be a cattle baron. You'll keep him right, Lizzie. Stop him squandering his inheritance. And I'll pay for the damage — some day.' Lizzie flounced back inside, the scowl once more in place, then quickly re-emerged to count the fowl.

'Feel bad about Annie. It was too bad we had a hand in taking out her brother.'

'Gorman was hell-bent on killing you, Pa. It had to be done.'

Jerem Chesney nodded in agreement.

'I guess you're right.'

'You and Lucas sure can pick the ladies.' Nathan's words and laughter broke the serious mood and Pa went out back to speak to Seb and John Grant.

'When are you guys leaving Flat Stone, Nathan?' asked Kaid.

'Soon as the Grants are ready to move out. Are you still set on torching the place?'

'Nope. I guess Jude'll want to keep his chickens out here. Maybe he'll try his hand at cooking, like he says he's so good at, and start a cook shop nearer the edge of the property, just off the trail. Flat Stone's expanding this way and he's ambitious. Reckon Jude and Lizzie will come up with something that makes them a fortune. It's my present to the kid.' They watched as the Grants began loading the buggy Seb had brought back that morning, duly cleansed and fumigated, as Pa headed on up to the rise.

The red dust kicked up by Kaid's

boots no longer seemed a threat. His eyes refused to look about at the land that had held them all prisoner for so long, especially Pa who'd had no real reason to be there in the first place. The sun was already high and the lone figure on the rise seemed somehow taller and stronger, his head no longer bowed under the weight of guilt, secrecy and sorrow. Kaid hesitated, unwilling to break the bond between the children and the only person other than himself who had truly loved them. But then he moved quietly ahead and looked at the marker he'd carved only days before.

'Guess that'll be the last marker needed.' As Kaid spoke, Pa pushed it further down into the dusty earth, firmly and securely. Their eyes met and Kaid turned and made his way slowly down off the rise.

'You're free, Kaid,' the voice called to him, 'free of everything and everyone. Got money coming to you. Use it to make up for the last fifteen years.'

Kaid shook his head. He wanted nothing that had been Rattigan's.

'Got no use for it. Belongs buried back there on the rise. They paid the price. I'll make my own way.' He waited till Pa came slowly up to him and they faced each other, alone for the first time that morning.

'Lizzie Grant's a real nice gal, clever too.'

'That she is, Pa, and she makes a real good friend. Strong-willed and knows her own mind. But it seems to me there could be a real danger in that and I've had enough of strong-minded women who think they're right all the time. There's no give in Lizzie, Pa, and that don't spell freedom to me.' Pa nodded. 'Guess I'll just drift for a bit. What about you? Going home to the Sephinas with Nathan and the boys?'

'That's where I belong, son, always have. It's all over now and you owe it to yourself to move on, Kaid, make life the way you want it. Reckon we can call it quits. Stay safe, son, and you know

286

where to find me if you need me.'

'I don't want that, Pa. It'll never be over between us. You and Nathan are the only kin who care. Reckon I'd like to tag along if you guys will let me. Got a notion to hear you sing 'Buffalo Gal' one more time.' Jerem Chesney laughed that infectious laugh of his and Kaid smiled broadly. His pa looked up at the high peaks of the Sephinas as he spoke.

'Son, there ain't no red dust up there. I give you my word.'

Pa's word would always be good enough for Kaid McEntyre.

THE END

VENGEANCE RIDES THE RIVER

Hugh Martin

The murder of Dave Lockhart's wife, by desperados who plague the Red River country of Texas, results in his desperate mission for revenge. Lockhart is no natural killer, but his quest for revenge becomes marked by murder, bullets and gun-smoke, and brings him face to face with deadly men. Then he meets Helen, who must overcome difficulties that few women ever face. Now she must teach Lockhart that there can be a world of difference between vengeance and justice . . .

DOC DRYDEN, GUNSLINGER

Ted Rushgrove

Clay Dryden, one of the band of outlaws known as the Sankey gang, is challenged to a gunfight by the brother of the gang leader and kills him. Finding that there were no bullets in his brother's revolver, Sankey vows to avenge his death. Then, in the town of Crossville, Sankey finds the former outlaw has set up a medical practice. Will Dryden be spared? It seems that Clay's future as the town's doctor hangs in the balance . . .